Samuel Parker and the New Templars

R. S. SEXTON

69

DEDICATION

To my lovely wife.

CONTENTS

ACKNOWLEDGMENTS

Artwork by: Gary McCluskey
http://garymccluskey.carbonmade.com/

1—CRAZY? AM NOT!

Quietly, Sam watched the orphans play. He longed to play tag or kickball—or even just talk to someone his own age. The chain-link fence and the bully held him back. The last time he caught their attention, the big kid called him *crazy*. His stomach panged, remembering the cruel laughter of the other orphans. He decided to stay on the bench.

Maybe he's right, he thought. After all, he had spent years in the C ward at the Sisters of Faith group home. The sisters sectioned part of the orphanage aside for difficult kids or, in his case, mentally disturbed.

He tried to think how long he'd been at the group home, but his medication fought against him. Twice a day, Sister Gertrude made him take his prescription. Sam tried telling Dr. Stiles the pills only made his brain go fuzzy, but he never listened.

"Don't you worry," he would say. "We're going to medicate those demons right out of you." Dr. Stiles didn't understand. Sam didn't have demons. He knew that for sure, because he could *see* demons.

His favorite time of day came after supper. The summer sun hung low, the orphans played, and his medication started to fade. *Five years.* He calculated, remembering his eleventh birthday. *I've been here five years.*

Sister Gertrude had recounted the story of how he arrived here several times. A homeless man had dropped him off and then disappeared. Sam had no memory of what happened, where he came from, or even who he was before that day. His only clue to his identity came on a torn piece of paper pinned to his Superman costume.

Samuel Parker
January 1, 2000

The sisters assumed the writing referred to his name and birthday. They tried finding his parents but eventually gave up.

Maybe I did come from another planet, like Superman.

As his medication continued to fade, the grass turned from its usual hazy gray to deep, rich shades of green. The excited, playful screams of kids rang clearly in his ears, as if he'd finally tuned in to the right station.

I wish I didn't have to take those stupid pills.

His sharpened senses gave him joy, but looming ever before him was his next pill. Sam knew his time was short, so he desperately inhaled the fragrance of the fresh-cut lawn, took in the bright colors of spring, and forced the sounds of playing kids deep into his memory. Although it hadn't worked yet, at least as far as he could remember, he hoped to recover at least part of these wonderful sensations after his next pill.

Out of the corner of his eye, he caught something moving. His play area looked nothing like the one across the fence. The other orphans played on swings, teeter-totters, and a merry-go-round. His playground consisted of a picnic bench, white gravel, and a six-foot chain-link fence. At the back of the pen sat a black dog. The dog raised a paw, as if saying hello. The attention felt good, even if from a dog. He waved back.

"Hello," a girl's voice issued from somewhere nearby. Sam looked around for the source but didn't find her. "I'm Abby, the black hound across the fence."

He heard angels and demons all the time—but never a talking dog. He checked his surroundings again for tricksters. Sometimes the other orphans could be cruel.

"Nobody else can hear me, so pretend you can't."

He understood *that* notion. People always freaked out when you heard things they couldn't.

"Please, come to the fence. I need to tell you something important." Abby barked and started wagging her tail.

All the orphans were busy playing, so Sam rose from the bench and walked the fifteen yards to the fence. It wasn't as if he had anything better to do. Even if it turned out to be a trick, at least someone took the time to do it. The black dog looked like a lab, except for her longer ears and, more impressive, her milky glow. Angels glowed the same way. He started to believe this wasn't a trick after all.

"I can read your thoughts, so don't say anything out loud. We don't want anyone thinking you're crazy."

Yeah, right. He chuckled in his misery.

"Everyone thinks you're crazy, but you're not. You know how you see angels and demons? Well, I'm sort of an angel."

So, nobody can see you? He dropped to his knees, sticking his fingers through the fence. Tiny gold flecks surrounded the edges of her dark eyes. When she licked his fingers, he smiled at the wetness of it. He'd never touched an angel before, not that he hadn't tried. His hands would go right through them, but not this time.

"Everyone can see me, but they can't hear me. I'm talking to you in your head. It's perfectly normal for a boy to like dogs, and you must act as normal as possible if we're going to get you out of here."

It took several years of counseling for Sam to realize he wasn't normal. When he first came to the home, the sisters thought his imaginary friends were cute. However, when he started repeating what the dark ones said, the sisters changed their minds. They separated him from the other orphans and brought in a doctor. From then on, they started giving him medication.

What are you going to do, tear down the fence? He grabbed the mesh and shook it.

"I could if I wanted, but breaking you out would cause too much commotion. What we need to do is make people think you're normal. You must stop telling people you can see the future and spirits. And you need stop taking those pills."

Good luck with that, he thought sarcastically. Sister Gertrude checks to make sure I swallow.

"How does she give it to you?"

She hands me a little paper cup with a pill. I throw the cup up, and the pill flies into my mouth. Sam gestured with his hand as if he were taking the pill. I've done it so long, I don't even need water. After I take the pill, I open wide and raise my tongue so she can check if I swallowed.

"Perfect. Next time, block the pill from going into your mouth. Use your lip or tongue, but make sure it stays in the cup. Pretend to swallow, and when she checks your mouth, pour the pill out in your other hand in case she checks the cup."

That might work. His thoughts grew very clear, and he liked how it felt.

Abby gave a muffled woof and shook her mane. "Here comes Sister Gertrude. I'll be staying in the timber behind me, so I'll always be close. If you need anything, just think it. I can hear anything you think." Abby bolted for the timber.

Sister Gertrude stood at the door and yelled, "Sam, it's time to come in."

"Remember, you must pretend to be normal." Although Abby had reached the timber, her voice stayed loud in his head. "And for heaven's sake, don't tell them about me."

He got up and grudgingly walked to the door. Sister Gertrude, short, round, and stern, waved her chubby hand for him to come. "Dr. Stiles is waiting." She held out the paper cup. "Here's your medication." She smiled, waiting for him to take it.

"Do it," Abby's voice echoed in his head.

He took the cup and flung it up to his mouth, but this time, he let the pill bounce off his top lip, back into the cup. He exaggerated the swallow and quickly opened wide for Sister Gertrude's inspection. Following Abby's instructions, he emptied the cup into his other hand, only he missed and the pill dropped to the ground. His heart throbbed from panic.

Abby yelled in his head, "Don't look down!"

He didn't, and Sister Gertrude steered him by the shoulder through the door. "You want to be careful of stray dogs. They might bite. Now hurry up. The doctor's waiting."

Sam smiled. She didn't even check the cup.

***

Dr. Stiles, portly, balding, and nervous, tugged at his scraggly beard importantly, as if thinking deep thoughts. As always, he sat in Sister Gertrude's office chair. Although not everyone had an angel or a demon, Dr. Stiles had both.

"Hello, Sam. Are we alone today?"

He always asked the same question, and the truthful answer was a resounding "no." Andy and Dean plainly stood on each side of Dr. Stiles.

Andy and Dean bickered constantly in their efforts to influence Dr. Stiles's behavior, but not once had they talked to Sam, so he didn't know their real names. Since he had seen them once a week for the last five years, he decided to name them.

"Yes, we're alone."

Dr. Stiles nodded his head grimly to his answer, like always. "What are they saying toda—" Stopping short of asking his usual second question, the doctor's heavily lidded eyes opened wide in apparent shock. Even Andy and Dean shot Sam surprised looks, which he forced himself to ignore.

"Oh, really?" Dean said, smirking at Andy. "I believe the young one has learned to lie. That's one for our side."

Andy heatedly replied, "Well, what can you expect? They drug him when he tells the truth."

Sam concentrated hard in order to block out their conversation. He focused all his attention on Dr. Stiles.

"Oh my goodness. I didn't expect that." Dr. Stiles unconsciously combed his hair over to hide his bald spot.

"After you finish with the liar, you should reward yourself by getting a double cheeseburger. Your extra weight only makes you more manly." Dean snickered as Dr. Stiles smacked his lips at his suggestion. Dean was always doing that, and sadly, Dr. Stiles tended to listen.

"Stop pretending you have hair," said Andy. "And you know better than to go off your diet. Your heart will explode if you don't get your weight under control."

Dr. Stiles's face flushed, and he stopped hiding his bald spot. "Have you taken your medication today?"

"Sister Gertrude gave me my pill before I came here." He didn't like how lying made his insides cringe. So, instead, he decided he would leave some parts out.

Dean chuckled. "Another point for our side. He's already learning to lie while speaking the truth. Advanced for his age. He might become a politician."

"You seem different today." Dr. Stiles peddled his chair with his fat legs to roll closer to him. "What do you think caused this sudden break into reality?"

"I don't know." Sam desperately thought back to his previous sessions. "I was outside thinking about our talks. I believe I had some traumatic accident at seven, which caused me to make stuff up. I'm sure I was only doing it for attention, like you said before, but now I understand. I think you fixed me."

"My lands. I did say that, didn't I? This is wonderful news," he said, leaning forward. "I wondered if I'd ever reach you, but here you are." His face turned sour, as if he'd bitten into a lemon. Reaching for his briefcase, he removed a stack of cards Sam recognized.

The dreaded inkblot test.

His "imaginary friends" weren't the only reasons everyone thought he was crazy. Seeing the future was another. He saw scenes in his head like a movie skipping forward a few seconds, but when his sight returned, they played out for real. At first, they popped up before something bad would happen, which confused him for a long time. Eventually, he figured out the first one was a warning, followed by the real thing. Over the years, he learned to turn his ability on and off at will. Unfortunately, he had shown Dr. Stiles his ability by predicting which inkblot card turned up next.

"OK, which card will I turn over?" Dr. Stiles asked with a tone of hope mixed with doubt.

"I don't know," Sam lied, shaking his head.

"Go ahead and guess."

Sam scrunched his forehead in fake concentration. "Maybe—the one with two people facing each other."

Dr. Stiles turned over the card with the butterfly and grinned. "Excellent."

Sam's big brown eyes stared innocently at the doctor. "But I got it wrong."

"Exactly." Dr. Stiles shoved the cards back into his briefcase. He jumped up and waddled out of Sister Gertrude's office to find her sitting outside. "Sister, sister!"

Sister Gertrude dropped her crochet to the floor and got up. "What's wrong?"

He beamed at her. "Nothing at all. He's cured. No future, no demons, no angels. I've cured him!"

"Cured?" Sister Gertrude twisted her face, as if she didn't understand.

"Yes, yes, I've seen this happen before. One day they're completely delusional, and the next, perfectly sane. I think I'll write up a case study. Oh, won't my colleagues be jealous? So exciting. I cured yet another one. He'll need to stay on his medication, of course, and I'll check on him for the next few months, but I'll bet anything he's cured."

Sister Gertrude caught on. "Oh, how wonderful." She peered at Sam's grinning face. "No angels or demons?"

Andy and Dean stood next to Dr. Stiles. "Nope, only you and the doctor."

Andy grinned, as did Dean. It was rare to see their expressions match.

Andy suspiciously glared at Dean. "Why are *you* smiling?"

"Our fat doctor added pride to his gluttony. That's an excellent combination, if I say so myself. Watch this." Dean leaned into Dr. Stiles's ear. "You should celebrate your genius by getting a triple cheeseburger. Victories like this don't happen every day."

Dr. Stiles's eyebrows rose, and his mouth opened in delight. "Sister, I'm going to celebrate Sam's breakthrough at the Burger Shack. Would you like to come?" Dr. Stiles danced into the hall as if he had ants in his pants. "I'm buying."

Andy rolled his eyes at Dean but then turned and gave Sam a wink. "I guess the other side wins this round." Sam could tell from the way the wry smile touched the angel's lips he was mocking Dean, but Sam didn't let on.

"Oh my," said Sister Gertrude, putting a hand to her mouth. "Let me drop Sam off first, and then we can go. I haven't had a real cheeseburger in ages."

Dean raised his fists in victory. "I'm on a roll. I got two gluttons for the price of one."

"We'll see," said Andy confidently. "By the time those two reach the restaurant, I'll make them feel so guilty they'll get salads."

Sam laughed.

Dr. Stiles and Sister Gertrude whipped their heads around in accusation, as if they'd caught Sam faking.

Sam shrugged his shoulders in apology. "I'm sorry. I'm just so happy to be normal."

The doctor and sister sighed with relief.

"Sister Gertrude?" Sam gave her a serious look.

She put a hand on his shoulder. "Yes?"

"Didn't Sister Gloria say eating cheeseburgers was like a sin?" Dean's smile drooped and Andy's turned up as if connected in reverse. Andy gave him a smirking nod.

"Mind your own business," she replied curtly, steering him down the hall by his shoulder. "Sister Gloria eats like a horse. She's only skinny because she has a high metabolism."

The anger in Sister Gertrude's face kept him from asking what she meant.

***

Dr. Stiles's few months turned into nine, but Sam didn't mind. Free from his mind-numbing medication, he possessed something he'd never experienced before. Hope. Abby kept him company always, inside or out. He did have to admit it was much better talking to her in person. At least then he could pet her through the fence. Having Abby to talk to felt almost like having a family. Well, as far as he knew, since he never had one before.

2—NEW KID ON THE BLOCK

The only thing Sam liked about his room was the window. It had a perfect view of the forest behind the home. He didn't have to see Abby to talk to her, but something about her dark figure next to the woods was comforting. He had spent countless hours staring out the window and talking to his only friend. He wondered if his new room would have the same view.

Abby emerged from the timber, staring in his direction. "All the boys have rooms in the back. I'm sure you'll still be able to see me from your new room."

Abby stood at least a hundred yards away, but she sounded close enough to touch. He smiled. Although, she told him countless times she would never leave him, he still feared she might disappear when he moved out of the C ward.

There you are. You're late. He grimaced when his tease rang too sharply.

Abby's head dropped. "Sorry, but Mrs. Wilson had sausage gravy with homemade biscuits this morning, and I couldn't pass it up. You know how hard it is for me to find good food. You don't expect me to rummage through the trash, do you?"

It was Sam's turn to duck his head. He tried to sneak her food, but it was hard to hide from Sister Gertrude's eagle eyes. *I was only kidding. It's just a big day.* He sighed with relief when Abby's tail wagged wildly.

"Moving in with the other orphans is a big step for us. We're almost home free now. I'm betting you'll get adopted soon, as long as you keep acting normal. Even if you make friends, don't let them know about your powers. They won't understand. And whatever you do, don't get into trouble."

Sam nodded his head in agreement but didn't have a chance to reply because someone walked through his door.

Sister Gertrude gave Sam an encouraging smile. "Are you ready?"

He grabbed his sack of clothes from his bed and took her outstretched hand. He trembled with excitement as she led him down the hall to the normal kids' block. The gray metal door at the end of the hallway had always separated him from the others. His stomach cartwheeled as she swiped her key card. The door clicked open.

"There are only three others your age: Mary, Roger, and Mike. Stick close to Mary. She's a good girl, and I told her to look out for you." She opened the door. "Watch out for Mike. He's a bit of a bully. If he gives you any problems, tell me. I'll take care of him."

He didn't know what to expect, but another empty hallway wasn't what he had in mind. She quickly dragged him into the first room on the right. The sparse room contained a dresser, wastebasket, and four neatly made beds.

Sister Gertrude pointed at the dresser. "You can put your clothes in the third drawer down."

He opened the empty drawer and neatly stacked his meager clothing. Once he shut the drawer, she pointed to one of the beds.

"That one is yours. The same rules apply as in your other room. You must make your bed before you leave the dormitory. Now for introductions." She grabbed his hand and led him out of his room.

"Sister Gertrude." He threw the empty sack in the trash as he passed by.

"Yes?"

He grimaced, afraid of hurting her feelings. "Do you have to hold my hand?"

She stopped to stare. "Afraid you'll appear weak?"

"Yeah," he replied, raising his eyebrows in apology.

"That's good thinking." She released her grip. "This way to the recreation room."

They passed several rooms like his. A few younger children eyed him with curiosity as he walked by. One brave boy even waved, which made Sam smile nervously.

"Here we are. Ready?" She grabbed the doorknob and waited for his nod. When she opened the door, three pairs of eyes focused on him. They were sitting around the TV.

"Hello, everyone. I'd like to introduce you to Sam." She began pointing at each one in turn. "Roger, Mike, and Mary."

"Hello, Sam," they said in unison, as if they had practiced.

"Hi," he replied.

Sister Gertrude's grin stretched her chubby cheeks. "I'll leave you to get acquainted." She left, shutting the door behind her.

Mary, brunette, pretty, and smiling, got up from the couch with her hand out. "Hi, Sam."

He shook her hand, surprised by her strong grip. She stood at least two inches taller than him, which made his insides squirm.

Roger struggled to get up from the threadbare couch. He finally managed to thrust free, but his momentum knocked the portly boy off balance. Luckily he regained his footing by grabbing one of the four metal poles that were dispersed around the open room. "Broken springs," he said sheepishly, sticking out his hand. Sam's hand disappeared into his. "My folks died in a car crash. I've been here almost two years."

Sam's smile faded. He couldn't remember his parents, and he didn't want to admit he had been here for six years. He hoped they wouldn't recognize him.

"Aren't you the loony kid?" Mike didn't bother to get up from the recliner, and by his expression, he already knew the answer to his question.

"Yeah, that's me, crazy." He attempted a smile through clenched teeth.

Mike pulled the lever on the chair so the footrest folded in. He leaned forward. "So, why'd they lock you up?"

Sam wanted to crawl in a hole.

Mary glared at Mike. "Don't be rude."

Mike was big, strong, and apparently cruel. When he stood up, he towered over Mary. "I think we have the right to know. I have to share a room with him."

Sam tapped on Mary's shoulder because she'd stepped between him and Mike. Her attempt to protect him from the bully warmed his heart. He felt like hugging her, but instead he winked and stepped around her to face the bully.

Mike scowled down at him. "Why'd they lock you up in the booby hatch?"

Thankful that Andy and Dean weren't there, he started lying. "Oh, I had a little misunderstanding with my big brother. He was about your size, come to think of it."

"Misunderstanding?" Mike's brows creased, which didn't help his appearance.

"My brother disappeared. I don't know why they blamed me. I liked Mike. Some called him a bully, but he was only playing. Hey, your name's Mike too. That's funny. You remind me of him. Well, there wasn't any proof, except for all that blood, but the cops stuck me in

13

here anyway." Mike involuntarily inched back, but Sam caught the retreat. He took the opportunity to turn to Mary. "Do we eat with metal forks and knives?"

Mary solemnly nodded, but she had a slight twinkle in her eyes. He guessed she caught on to his joke, but Roger backed to the door. "Can't blame them, though. It did look bad when my parents died in the house fire." When he clapped his hands, Mike jerked back a step. "It's good to be free, but I hope they don't mess my meds up again. When it's wrong, I go *crazy*." He grinned and opened his eyes wide, hoping he looked disturbed.

Mike's face turned pale, and he darted from the room.

Before Roger could do the same, Sam called out, "Stop."

Roger froze in his tracks and slowly turned his head.

"I played a joke on Mike. I made that stuff up. Sorry if I scared you." Sam grinned at him.

Roger's round face scrunched in confusion for a moment, and then he smiled. "Knew it the whole time. Mike sure took off. You really got him good."

"You better be careful," said Mary. "He has a bad temper, and if he finds out you lied, he'll fight you. He won't have the nerve when I'm around because I'll report him, but I won't always be around."

Sam grinned. "I have a few tricks up my sleeve. Don't worry about me." He'd never been in a fight before, but seeing the future had to help. "Kind of looking forward to it."

***

An hour later, the three were sitting cozily on the couch, watching a show the sisters wouldn't approve of. Plainly, the other two were thinking the same thing because they jumped almost as high as he did when the door burst opened.

"Hah! You're a liar," said Mike, stomping in. "You didn't kill your brother or your parents. Sister Margret

SAMUEL PARKER AND THE NEW TEMPLARS

wouldn't tell me why you were in the nuthouse, but she said you didn't kill anyone."

Roger hadn't been kidding about the couch springs. Sam sat in a hole, which made him feel even smaller as Mike towered over him.

Mike clenched his fists. "I ought to knock your block off. Just you wait until we go to bed. I'll teach you to lie to me."

"Back up and I'll give you a chance right now." Sam didn't know why he grinned because he shook like a leaf on the inside.

To make matters worse, Abby started yelling in his head. "You can't get into trouble. They'll send you back for fighting!"

Mike glanced at Mary. "I would, but she would tattle-tell on me."

Mary started to speak, but Sam grabbed her arm. His words were also for Abby. "Like the sisters say, have a little faith. I would rather do this now than later." He lightly squeezed Mary's arm. "Promise Mike you won't tell on him."

Worried creases appeared on her forehead. "Mike's so much bigger than you. I can't."

"Typical. Boys always use their fists when they should be using their words. You're smarter than this!" Abby's scold pinched his chest. He could feel the heat rising up through his shirt, but he continued staring at Mary.

"You won't be in our room later, so it's going to happen anyway." Sam forced a grin. "I promise I won't hurt him. Have a little faith."

Mary pursed her lips tight and glared up at Mike. "I do have faith. I won't tell on you. Now back away so Sam can get up."

Mike laughed and backed into a fighting stance. His fists were already weaving about his chin when Sam stood up. "I won't mess your face up *too* bad."

Sam moved from the couch. He needed some room. Finding a good open area, he stood straight up with his feet shoulder length apart. "OK, anytime you're ready." He gave his most confident face, but by Mary's worried expression, he probably failed.

"You're making this too easy. I bet I knock you out with one punch." Mike stepped in and punched. Instead of connecting to Sam's chin, he hit only air.

Sam grinned in relief as Mike regained his balance. His ability to see the future allowed him to step easily out of the way.

"You're fast for a crazy runt. Try to stop this." Mike closed the distance again, but this time he jabbed with his left, punched with his right, and then tried kicking Sam in the stomach. Nothing even came close to connecting.

Sam yawned as if he were bored. "Like I said, you can start anytime."

Mike came with a fury of punches and kicks that lasted until he could go no longer. Sam easily dodged each attempted blow. Mike bent over with his hands on his knees, gasping for breath and glaring.

Sam saw the next attack coming. Mike launched into a sprint with his arms opened wide for a tackle. At the right moment, Sam stepped aside. The metal pole rang like a gong when Mike's head crashed into it. The big brute fell to the floor like a wet noodle. Sam immediately turned to Mary. "I didn't hurt him. He hurt himself."

She nodded in agreement. "I need to go tell someone. He might have really hurt himself." Off like a flash, she left the room.

"Holy smokes, you're fast." Roger walked up to Mike's limp body. He lightly kicked Mike's leg and then jumped back. "Serves you right, you big bully." He jumped back even farther when Mike groaned.

Sam didn't want to go back to the mental ward for fighting. "I never touched him."

"Don't worry. I saw the whole thing. He tried to fight, but you kept dodging him. Man, you're *fast*."

Sam grinned wide when Abby decided to speak again. "I take it back. You're a genius."

***

In the end, everything had turned out perfectly. Not only had Mary and Roger told the same story, Mike had even confirmed what had happened. His woozy confession had sealed his fate. Sister Gertrude had praised Sam for not fighting, and Mike had gotten a week in the booby hatch.

3—WINDOW SHOPPING

Abby's black fur felt warm from the afternoon sun, like a blanket straight from the dryer. Sam almost moaned with pleasure when he hugged her. The best thing about the normal kids' playground was that it wasn't fenced in. Although he played with the other kids, today he wanted to sit on the grass with Abby. Nobody stood nearby, so he talked aloud. "Well, what do you think my chances are?"

Abby groaned as Sam scratched under her chin. "You'll get picked today." She gave him a huge hound smile with her tongue hanging out.

Sam stifled a laugh. "You sound like you know for sure. Sister Gertrude told us not to get our hopes up."

"She might be right most of the time, but not for you. You're getting new parents today."

Sam desperately wanted to believe her, but common sense kept getting in the way. "Mary, Roger, and Mike have gone through this a bunch of times, and they're still here. I understand why nobody would want Mike, but Mary? I doubt I get picked my first time out."

Abby playfully swiped her tongue across his face. "Trust me, today is the day."

Sam laughed as he wiped her slobber off his face, but then his smile faded.

Mike stood a few yards away, smirking and holding a red rubber ball. "Hey, look, everyone. Nutsy is talking to that stupid mutt. I told you he's still crazy." The bully looked around for approval from the few kids looking in his direction, but they quickly went back to playing.

Abby gave a low growl and bared her teeth, but Sam jumped to his feet, smiling. "You better be careful who you call stupid. She doesn't like it."

The hair on the back of her neck sprang up menacingly as she stepped forward, growling.

Mike's eyes widened as he took a step back. "How does she know I called her stupid? That's some sort of trick. You're making her do that. Stop her or I'll tell."

"I don't think I can control her, but if you say you're sorry and tell her she's smart, she might not rip off your entire leg."

Mike's eyes flitted back and forth between Sam and Abby as he weighed his choices, but when Abby took another step, he reacted. "OK, sorry. And I think you're smart."

Mike's jaw dropped in shock as Abby calmly sat down and smiled.

Sam laughed as Mike cautiously backed away. "You know, we could probably be the best circus act in the entire world. You could do any trick without being trained."

Abby stiffened and turned toward Sam. "You're forgetting something. Just because you want me to do a dog trick, doesn't mean I'll do it."

He bent down and scratched behind her ears in apology. "I didn't mean it that way. I was just saying we make a good team."

She gave him another big swipe of her tongue, laughing as he wiped his face. "I know, silly boy. I was just yanking your chain."

***

"Comb that mess. They'll be here in less than twenty minutes. You want to make a good impression, don't you?" Sister Gertrude spat in her chubby hand and began shellacking his unnatural cowlick.

Sam saw her coming way before her assault, but he held still. After all, what was a little spit if it helped get him parents? His head buzzed with excitement as he tried to keep his knees from buckling under her heavy-handed strokes.

She sighed in her failure to get his hair in order. "Here, take your pill. We don't want a relapse today of all days."

He took the small paper cup she extended and pretended to take his medication.

After she inspected his mouth, she nodded and patted his head encouragingly. "Don't be too disappointed if you don't get picked your first time out." Her smile stretched her puffy cheeks. "We'll be bringing perspective parents into the viewing room at two," she said, gesturing at the clock on the wall and pointing at the one-way mirror.

"If they like what they see, I'll come get you for an interview, so please do something...they like." Her unwavering smile didn't match the sadness in her eyes. "Have a little faith."

Sam expertly dropped the pill back into the container while everyone watched her leave. He casually chucked the wadded paper cup into the wastebasket by the door.

"Man, I wish I had pills," said Roger, staring at the mirror. His round belly made tucking in his shirt difficult. Roger was large, slow, and sensitive. He was always chosen last for games, and he usually cried whether his team won or lost. Once satisfied his shirt was picture perfect, he wiped the beads of sweat from his forehead, causing his shirt to come loose. "Maybe if I had medicine, I wouldn't be so nervous."

Mary stopped Roger from pulling something out of his pocket. No doubt food he'd stored from lunch. "Don't be silly. You'll be fine."

"Yeah, tubby, I'm sure there's a fat couple waiting to adopt a porker like you." Mike's attitude hadn't changed much since his injury, but he stayed clear of Sam. He leaned his chair back in a satisfied manner, grinning at Roger's tears.

"Unkind behavior stems from insecurities," Mary said, quoting one of the lines they heard countless times in counseling. Her face turned red, but she continued in a controlled manner as she rubbed soothingly on Roger's back. "Mike's only scared you'll be picked first and with good reason. I'd pick you over *that* bully any day."

The sting of her words made Mike jerk, causing his chair to slip out from under him. He hit the floor hard. Enraged, he instantly sprang to his feet to face Mary.

Sam never moved a muscle, except to form the slightest hint of a smile. He gleefully watched the exchange. Mary had taken him under her wing since his release from the mental ward last month. She was kind, but gritty. Sam learned a lot about the power of words from her example. She could whip anyone back in place with her biting wit. Sam wouldn't hesitate for a second to stop Mike from hurting her, but he knew the bully would back down.

Seeing the future wasn't like in the movies where a fortune-teller might only get some things right. Sam's visions were never wrong. Granted, he only saw a few seconds at a time, but that showed Sam enough to know Mike would breathe heavy, glare at Mary, and then pick up his chair to sit down. And that's exactly what he did. Unlike Sam, Mary didn't know what Mike would do, but she never backed down. Sam smiled at her nerve.

He glanced at the clock—seven minutes to kill. He noticed Roger starting to dig into his pockets again, so he grabbed his arm. "Hey, wanna see a cool card trick?" Mary flashed a smile as he dragged Roger over to the table. He grinned back at her. "You might like this too. Come sit down. I've been saving this for a special occasion."

The observation room contained only one long table set lengthwise to the one-way mirror, four chairs, and the wastebasket by the door. Sam removed a deck of cards from his pocket and sat next to Mike. He figured nobody would want to sit by the bully.

He handed Roger the deck. "OK, shuffle these all you want. When you're ready, put twelve cards facedown in three rows."

Roger's brow furrowed.

"Three rows with four cards each," suggested Sam.

Roger smiled. "Gotcha." He shuffled seven times, cut the deck once and then laid out three rows of cards. "Now what?"

Sam smiled. "I'm going to tell you the number and suit of the card you'll turn over."

"How ya gonna do that?" Roger frowned in doubt.

"You'd be surprised at the tricks you learn in the loony bin."

"Humph!" Mike crossed his arms and tipped back in his chair, but then cautiously set the chair back down.

Ignoring the bully, Sam grinned at Roger. "OK, are you ready?"

Roger nodded and shot a doubtful glance over at Mary.

"Let me concentrate." He put his hand on his forehead, moaning in an outlandish way. "I have it. You'll turn over the four of diamonds."

"That's stupid, there's no way—" started Mike, but stopped short when Roger turned over the four of diamonds.

Roger's jaw dropped and Mary giggled.

"How'd you do that?" Roger's excited face turned a brighter shade of pink than normal.

"Good card trick, huh? Well, come on. Let's do another." Sam put his hand on his forehead and started moaning, but this time he swayed back and forth for good measure. "Queen of spades."

Roger smirked when he hovered his hand over one card and then suddenly picked another, turning over the queen of spades. "Well, I'll be."

Sam chuckled at Roger's amazement.

Mike leaned in closer. "Those are trick cards. I bet they're marked or something."

Mary crossed her arms and raised an eyebrow. "Even if they were marked, how would he know which one Roger would pick?"

"They're in it together. I bet booby hatch boy couldn't do it if I put the cards down."

Mary leaned in to reply, but Sam raised his hand. "This trick is pretty hard, but if you think the cards are marked, I'll make you a bet. I bet I can tell you what card turns up when you cut the deck. If I guess right, you have to do all our chores for a month. If I'm wrong, I'll do your chores for three months." He thought about making Mike swear to quit being a jerk, but he knew better than to ask for the impossible.

Mike leaned in with greedy eyes. "And I want your desserts for three months."

"Done. Are you ready?" Sam would have agreed to anything since he couldn't lose.

"You're such a sucker," said Mike, holding his hand over the deck.

"You'll cut the deck on…" He smiled. "There is no number or suit, but the card fits you. You'll pick the fool card, the joker."

Mike moved his fingers up and down several times before settling on a place to cut the deck. His face turned sour when he turned over the joker. "I don't know how you cheated, but I'm not doing your chores, and *nobody* can make me. Besides, I'm going to get picked today, so it doesn't matter anyway. With a fat crybaby, a goody two-shoes, and a psycho, the chances you three get picked are zilch. Hah, never gonna happen."

"Somehow, I knew you were going to say that." Sam laughed, but what made him laugh was the time. It was five minutes past two. Any parent at the window just witnessed Mike being a jerk. He had no doubt Sister Gertrude heard him because his ability showed her coming through the door, and she was hopping mad.

The door flew open so fast a gust of wind blew across the room, making them all jump. Even Sam acted surprised.

Sister Gertrude pressed her lips so thin, her words barely escaped her mouth, but there was no mistake Mike was in *trouble*. "Michael, please come with me." He'd barely left the view of the one-way mirror when she jerked him from the room by the ear.

Roger checked the time. Sam could almost see the cogs turning in his head. Desperately, Roger gestured, using his eyebrows and head to warn Mary about the time.

She sweetly smiled and put a hand on his arm. "Good luck."

His face reddened, and his eyes welled.

"Oh, please, Roger, don't. Have a little faith like Sister Gertrude said," whispered Mary. She then spoke a little louder than normal, but not obviously louder. "I'm sure you'll find the perfect parents because you are a good boy. You are loving, thoughtful, and sweet. If I were to choose a son, I'd choose you."

I didn't need a gift to predict that one, thought Sam. Mary always thought of others first. It's probably why she's still here, but what happened next did surprise him.

Roger got up and didn't pretend he was talking to anyone but to the people on the other side of the glass. "Mary is the sweetest, kindest, most giving person I know. There are two kinds of people in this world, givers and takers. If you want a taker, he just left the room. If you want a giver, her name is Mary, and she's standing right here." Roger gazed into the mirror as if he could see through to the people on the other side. Slowly, his eyes focused on his own reflection, and by his expression, maybe for the first time, he liked what he saw.

There wasn't a dry eye in the room. Even Sam's eyes got a little glassy. Roger was more than right, and if anyone deserved a family, it was Mary, so Sam stepped up beside Roger. "Mary's a good friend, super smart, funny, and…and…well, she's pretty." He teasingly punched Roger in the shoulder. "Dude, you got all the good ones."

Roger chuckled and playfully punched him back. "Nah, man, yours were good."

They both turned to find Mary softly sobbing with her head in her hands. They grabbed her by the arms and put her up to the glass. She wouldn't raise her head, but Sam did.

"Seriously, if you don't pick her, you don't deserve her."

Roger nodded in agreement.

"And if you have any sense at all, you'll take Roger too."

Roger smiled and started to face the glass again, but Sam cut him off in a whisper. "I don't think I'm ready to leave yet. We don't want to ruin Mary's chances."

Roger paused, staring at him for a moment before it registered. He nodded. "How about some more card tricks? I think I might figure it out this time."

Sam smiled and headed for the table. He actually lied when he said he wasn't ready to leave. He'd been trapped here for six years. Not that he remembered much because of the drugs, but he knew there was a better life out there. There just had to be.

After ten minutes of card tricks, the three twelve-year-old orphans eagerly looked up to the opening door.

4—PACKAGE DEAL

Sister Gertrude's half-formed smile didn't bode well. Although she looked much happier than when she yanked Mike from the room, the rest of her screamed bad news.

"Unfortunately, we had only one couple today. You have to realize the difficulty of placing older children. Everyone wants babies. Anyway, I want to commend you for your actions today. I'm so proud of you. I know it's not fair, and I'm so sorry, but they only want to interview one."

Sam's stomach clenched so tight it squeezed his heart up to his throat. *Please let it be me.*

"Mary and Roger, you may go back to the dormitory. Sam, come with me."

His heart leaped, but just as quickly, the joy disappeared. He hoped she'd call his name, but he wasn't as happy as he should've been. It didn't help matters when Mary popped up to give him a hug.

"Oh, Sam, I'm so happy for you."

Her smile was real, but also her tears. Mary had endured this for three years, and this was his first try. *That has to hurt.*

Roger smiled and patted him on the back. "Way to go, buddy. We'll get picked next time."

Sister Gertrude gave each one a consoling pat as they walked by. They acted brave, but both wiped their eyes as they headed down the hall.

"Let's not keep them waiting, dear." Sister Gertrude gestured for him to come forward. "They seem like a nice couple." She spat in her hand and started working on his cowlick. "I told them about your earlier problems, so don't be afraid to answer their questions. Be polite." She grabbed him by the shoulders. "I don't want to scare you, but—I was serious about everyone wanting babies. We rarely get couples willing to take kids your age, so do your best. This interview might be your only chance for a family."

He only nodded, because his throat was too dry to speak. She led him to her office. The butterflies in his stomach grew to a flock of birds.

Sister Gertrude dragged him through her office door. "This is Sam Parker. Sam, this is Mr. and Mrs. Prawn."

"Hello, Sam," they said together.

"Hello," said Sam, barely above a whisper. His tense muscles relaxed when he noticed neither one had spirits beside them.

"I'll leave you three to get acquainted." Sister Gertrude pushed him forward so she could shut the door.

Mr. Prawn was ruggedly handsome and wearing a suit that appeared too tight for his muscles. Although clean-shaven, the lower part of his face was a shade lighter, as if he had recently shaved off a beard. He wasn't necessarily happy-looking, but not unpleasant, either.

Sam shook his strong and rough hand.

"You can call me Eli," he said, releasing his grip.

Mrs. Prawn, black hair pulled up tight in a bun, extremely thin, and frowning, didn't offer her long-fingered hand.

Sister Gertrude's office had a desk and chair to the left and an open area on the right where two chairs faced another chair. The Prawns took their seats and he took his.

"Let's not waste time." Eli leaned forward with concern. "Oh my, I think you might have something in your eye. My wife is a doctor. Do you mind if she checks?"

Sam brought a hand up to his face and started blinking. "I don't feel anything."

Mrs. Prawn opened her purse and removed what looked like a magnifying glass with a light. She put the device up to his eye for only a second. "Birthmark, nothing to worry about."

"Oh," said Sam, realizing what they'd seen. "Yeah, I've always had that red speck."

"OK, everything's perfect. We want you to come live with us. What do *you* say?" Eli leaned forward expectantly.

Sam stared at the couple, stunned. He had learned a long time ago, if it sounded too good to be true, it probably was. "Don't you want to know anything about me?"

Mrs. Prawn abruptly got up, walked to Sister Gertrude's desk, and returned with a folder. A thick folder, he noted, as she sat down and started flipping through the pages. "We have examined your records thoroughly. A homeless man dropped you off here when you were seven." She glanced a moment at her husband, as if she thought something was funny. She didn't smile, but her frown lightened. "You had a head injury that took your memory. For the next five years, you tried to convince the staff you had visions of spirits and the future. During that time, they used medication and counseling in the attempt to convince you otherwise. About a year ago, as the records show, you started recovering from your delusions and are now ready for adoption." She shut the folder sharply. "Is that about it?"

This harsh lady summed up his entire life in less than a minute. What surprised him was that she didn't seem bothered at all. "Umm…sounds about right." He definitely wouldn't say anything different.

Eli slapped his knee and smiled. "I guess we're all set, then. We have to do some paperwork, and you can leave with us in about a month."

This all happened too fast for Sam. He was supposed to ask questions, but what were they? He remembered Sister Gertrude reading off a list, but he hadn't paid attention. They all seemed dumb at the time. He did have one question though. "How come you don't care about me being crazy?"

Eli's smile faded. "Boy, we don't care what they believe. If you told *us* you saw spirits, *we* would believe you instead of filling you with drugs. We want to give you a better life than you have here, a much better life."

Sam was sold. "OK, but can I ask one favor? I'll never ask for anything ever again. I'll do whatever you want, I'll be the best boy in the world, I—"

Eli raised his meaty hand for him to stop. "I owe you at least that much. What's your favor?"

Sam didn't know what he meant by owing, but he wouldn't press his luck by asking. "Will you please adopt Mary and Roger too? They are super good kids." Sam pressed his lips tight and strained with hope. *Please say yes, please, please.* Only Eli started shaking his head.

Mrs. Prawn slapped her husband's leg to stop him from answering. "We can't take them in, but I promise you I'll find each of them a new home before we take you home. And rest assured, I'll find Mary and Roger exceptional parents who will love and take care of them properly." She sat back, satisfied, but still clung to her frown. "I have some pretty good connections."

"Then it's settled," said Eli, getting up. "I'll go get Sister Gertrude so we can start the paperwork." He put his hand on top of Sam's head. "I'm glad you will come live with me, us, but Sister Gertrude said the paperwork might take a month. We will be staying here in Little Rock, so we'll come visit you every day if you want."

The heat of Eli's hand radiated from Sam's head to his toes. He nodded with a smile.

"You can go tell your friends the good news about Penny finding them a family. When she makes a promise, you can bet your life it will happen."

Sam sprinted to the rec room, with a few jumps of joy along the way, but when he got to the door, he put on his saddest face. Just as he thought, Mary and Roger were waiting for him inside.

"Oh, Sam." Mary's cheerful face turned to concern. "What's wrong?"

"Well, I met with them and they wanted me."

Roger ambled over to him. "But why do you look so sad? Isn't that good news?"

"I asked for them to adopt you two also." Sam dropped his gaze to the floor in a sad way.

Mary put a hand on his shoulder. "And they said no, but they're still taking you, right?"

He sadly nodded his head. "They did say no, and yes they still want me, but I'm going to miss both of you so much. Do you guys promise to write me?"

Mary's sweet smile gave him a twinge of guilt. "I'll write, but you shouldn't have tried to get them to take us. You might've made them mad."

Roger patted him on the back. "Yeah, I'll write, and thanks for trying. You're a good friend."

Sam started to grin. "Make sure you tell me your new addresses so my letters go to the right places."

Mary's eyes narrowed. "New addresses?"

The good news burst out of Sam "They promised me they'd find each of you a home!"

"Shut up!" Mary pushed him back in excitement. "Serious?"

Roger's mouth gaped in silent shock.

"It's true," said Sam, beaming. "Mrs. Prawn said she had connections and you guys would get great parents. She promised, and Mr. Prawn said when she promises, you can bet your life it will happen."

Mary squealed and started jumping up and down. Without a word, Roger stepped forward and hugged him tightly. *This is the best day ever*, thought Sam.

***

True to her word, Penny didn't waste any time finding families for Mary and Roger. But he found out she didn't like to be called by her first name. She preferred Dr. Prawn, even by her own husband, which was strange. Eli came every day, but Dr. Prawn only showed up once in a while. Sam figured she was busy finding parents for Mary and Roger. When she did show up, she would give updates of her progress. By the end of the second week, she had lined up three families for Mary, two for Roger, and one family that wanted them both. Even Sister Gertrude admitted how unusual it was for orphans to choose their parents.

***

Sam sat in the backseat of a red four-door pickup heading for the mountains of Virginia. He looked through the back glass and smiled at the waving orphans, but mainly because Abby sat next to him.

He asked last week if she could go, and Eli had said yes right away. However, Dr. Prawn's usual frown had deepened when he had asked. Thankfully, she hadn't argued, but it was plain she hadn't liked the idea.

When they reached the outskirts of the city, Eli and Dr. Prawn exchange glances. Eli hit a button on his door and then caught Sam's eye in the rear-view mirror. "Don't get worried, but I childproofed your doors. You can't unlock them or roll down the window."

Sam wondered why that should worry him. He started getting an uncomfortable pang in his stomach as if he were about to hear bad news.

"Sam, we lied."

5—DECEPTION REVEALED

Panic shot through Sam like a bolt of lightning. *They lied. But what about? He locked me in. This can't be good.*

Eli kept glancing at the mirror while Dr. Prawn continued to stare out the windshield, unmoving.

Sam thought about trying to punch his window to escape, but his ability showed him if he tried, it would only hurt his hand.

Eli smiled in a reassuring way. "It's not as bad as it sounds. We didn't lie to hurt you. We lied to help you."

Sam wasn't comforted. The demon used the same type of logic on Dr. Stiles. "If it's not bad, why'd you lock me in?"

"I didn't want you jumping out before I told you the whole truth. I'll take you back to the group home if you want, but not before I say my piece."

"It's OK," said Abby, giving him a lick. "It's not bad at all."

He gave Abby an accusing stare, but didn't want to give away he could talk to her, so he thought his question instead. *How do you know?*

"I was in on it."

A cold sweat broke out over his skin. Feelings of treachery prompted him to remove his arm from around Abby.

Dr. Prawn sharply turned her head to Eli. "Did you really need to start all this before you dropped me off?"

Sam stared at Eli's reflection in the mirror. "Drop her off?"

Eli scowled at her. "He needs to understand we're not married before you leave."

"You guys aren't married?"

Both immediately turned around and, with notable conviction in their voices, said, "No!"

Sam jumped back in his seat.

Eli turned back around to drive. "We had to pretend to be married so we could adopt you. You and Abby will be living with me at my cabin. Dr. Prawn lives in DC"

"Thank heavens I won't have to smell that dog for fifteen hours." Dr. Prawn pointed frantically at the exit sign. "Don't miss your turnoff."

"You're not helping. Shut up or I'll make you walk to the airport." Eli's eyes narrowed into a serious glare. There was no doubt he meant what he said.

Dr. Prawn scowled, crossed her arms, and started staring out the windshield again.

Although Sam was still panicky, the thought of Dr. Prawn not being his new mom was somewhat soothing. She wasn't the most pleasant person in the world, and she didn't like dogs.

"You've been doing a little deceiving of your own. You stopped taking your medication, right?"

Sam didn't say anything.

"You can still see the future. That was plain enough when you picked out all the right cards. I'm betting you can still see angels and demons. So, don't be too quick to judge us."

He still didn't say anything, but his stomach unclenched a bit.

"I can see the future like you." Eli watched him through the mirror. "I don't see angels and demons, but I can talk to Abby." Eli's attention went to driving as he pulled up to the airport drop-off.

Sam had an idea. *When he lets out Dr. Prawn, I'll jump out too.*

Eli glanced at Sam in the mirror. "I can unlock the front doors without releasing the back doors."

Sam's brow furrowed.

Eli shrugged his shoulders. "Abby told me."

Sam gave Abby a look of betrayal as Dr. Prawn got out and slammed the door.

Eli lowered the passenger window and yelled after her. "Hey, what about your luggage?"

She never turned around, but yelled back in reply, "Burn them. I'll never get the dog stench out anyway." She disappeared through the glass doors of the airport.

Eli put the truck in drive, chuckled, and shook his head. "Man, she's a piece of work." He drove a little while without speaking as he maneuvered the pickup back to the interstate. "OK, I'll give you the short version. You believe in God, right?"

Sam shrugged his shoulders. "Kind of hard not to when you see angels and demons."

"God gave you powers just as He gave me powers. You're special. You know the red speck in your eye?"

"Yeah."

"Well, I have one too." Eli leaned closer to the mirror and shoved up his eyelid with a finger.

Sam almost came out of his seat. Eli's speck looked like his and in the same place. "Are we related?"

Eli frowned. "Sort of, but mainly we're a lot alike. I'm getting sidetracked. Let's go back to the beginning. Your ability is called chazah. I'm guessing your visions only last a few seconds, right?"

Sam nodded.

"Well, I can do that too, but there are different types of chazah. I get visions of the future that I must make happen. I call those tasks. I've been doing tasks for a long time. Have you had anything like that happen to you?"

Sam shook his head.

"I didn't think so, but you probably will when you get a little bigger. Well, one of those visions showed me I needed to be in a certain place and time so I could save you from a plane crash. You were seven. After I saved you, to complete my task, I had to take you to the Sisters of Faith group home and leave you there. I was the homeless guy they told you about. I didn't want to turn you over to them, but I didn't have a choice. Terrible things happen when I don't make my visions come true. Trust me."

"What about my parents?" Hope welled up in Sam like a tidal wave.

"I'm sorry, but your parents were never found."

"But if they were never found, they might still be alive." Sam's voice pleaded with hope.

Eli sadly shook his head. "If they haven't turned up by now, I doubt they made it."

"Why didn't you save them too?" he said accusingly.

"You need to understand, I didn't even know I was saving you. I just did what the vision showed me and when I finished, there you were, Superman costume and all."

Sam started to believe. He remembered the costume. For the first few months at the group home, that's all he wanted to wear.

"Penny had her own vision, and just as I saved you from the fall, she showed up. Good thing she did because you had a pretty bad head injury."

"She fixed my head?"

"Yes, but her schooling didn't save you. She has the gift of healing. She put her hand on your wound, and it instantly healed."

Eli's story sounded crazy, but he was used to crazy. "Did you know my parents?"

"Not personally, but they were good people. I'll show you their pictures when we get home."

I wasn't ditched. The news was good and bad at the same time. His parents didn't abandon him, but they were dead. He'd hoped they'd somehow lost him and one day he would find them, but now his dream was gone. *At least Eli has pictures.* "Why do you want me now, but didn't back then?"

Eli's fierce gaze made Sam push back in his seat. "Get one thing straight. I never wanted to leave you. When Abby told me they had you on medication, I wanted to tear the place apart, but I couldn't. My vision showed me leaving you with the sisters. I tried going against my visions once. I thought I had a better plan than God's. My plan led to death. Unfortunately, it wasn't mine."

Sam wondered who died, but Eli's eyes turned red and kept Sam from asking.

"Sometimes, we go through bad things so we'll be ready for what's to come. Your stay at the Sisters of Faith group home might not have been fun, but what you went through made you into the person you are today. I'm sorry you had to go through that, but I'm glad I waited. Last year, I had another vision to send you Abby."

This news made him forget he was mad at her. He put a hand on her head. "How long have you known her?"

"Her whole life. She stayed with me until last year when she came to help you. Now hold on to your shorts, I got a really big one to tell you. Ready?"

After what he had already heard, Sam doubted if anything Eli had to say would surprise him, but he nodded his head anyway.

"All our birthdays are on January 1st."

Sam pursed his lips in disappointment. "Lots of people have the same birthdays. That's no big deal."

"Yeah, but yours is exactly two thousand years after mine."

Sam's eyes narrowed.

Eli's chuckle turned into a laugh. "Of all the things I've told you, this is what you get stuck on? I haven't aged a day since I was thirty-seven years old. You will believe me in time. I just wish I stopped aging when I was twenty-five." He squirmed in his seat. "If I had, I doubt my butt would get this sore."

Sam turned to Abby. "Is that true?"

She raised her head. "Absolutely. Eli's butt gets sore all the time."

Sam laughed. "No, I mean is he that old?"

"I was created the second you were born, so I wasn't there, but I can vouch for him not aging for the last twelve years."

"Twelve is old for a dog." He looked for gray hairs, but couldn't find any.

"I'm not exactly a dog. My age is tied to yours, so picture me as a twelve-year-old girl trapped in this awesome dog's body."

Sam shuddered at the thought. "I didn't think angels aged."

"I'm not exactly an angel, either."

"If you're not a dog or an angel, then what are you?"

"I'm your shamar."

"Shamar?"

"A shamar guards something from evil. In my case, I'm your shamar. My life is connected to yours. If you die, I die."

"What happens if you die first?"

"Nothing. Well, nothing other than me dying."

"That doesn't seem fair." Sam scratched her behind the ears. She leaned into his hand and groaned with pleasure.

"I wouldn't want to live without you, so I think it's totally fair."

"Hey, I'm the one telling the story here." Eli leaned close to the mirror, frowning. The truck swerved a little into the other lane, and a car honked. He quickly swerved back.

Abby glanced out the window at the car they almost hit. "You better pay attention to the road before we all die."

Eli gave her a quick glare. "You two might, but I won't."

"Good point."

"Huh?" Sam frowned in confusion.

Eli dropped his head a bit. "OK, here goes nothing. I've been fighting evil for almost two thousand years. I've been stabbed, poisoned, beheaded, gutted, dismembered, blown up, drowned, shot, and even got myself burned at the stake once. I can't die."

"Holy smokes!" exclaimed Sam. "That's cool!"

Eli slowly shook his head, as if he disagreed. "It gets old after a couple hundred years." He seemed to be in a hurry to change the topic. "The red speck in your eye is a cross. The same cross I used when I started the Knights Templar. Penny spotted your birthmark when she healed your head. I knew the moment she showed me your cross you were my replacement."

"Replacement for what?" Sam asked, still confused.

"You will become the new Grand Master of the Knights Templar." Eli grinned in the mirror like that should mean something. "Good gracious, boy, didn't those nuns teach you anything?"

Sam shrugged his shoulders. "But if you can't die, why do you need a replacement?"

Eli paused for a long time, staring out the windshield. The silence of the pickup cab made Sam's head throb, not to mention the queasy feeling in his stomach as if he'd asked a very personal question.

Eli cleared his throat. "You have to understand I'm really old. I don't know for sure why or even how you will replace me, but it's something I've wanted for a long time. I'm hoping, when you're ready to take over, God will release me from this life."

The thought of Eli dying made Sam's stomach lurch. "I don't want to be the Grand Master if you die."

Eli smiled in the mirror. "It's not like it's going to be tomorrow. You still need to be trained, and I'm the only one who can do it. Besides, I don't even know whether that's the case. You may become the new Grand Master without me getting my wish." Eli nodded his head as if he wanted to change the subject. "OK, here's a lesson on history. Of course, my version is the only accurate account, since I was there."

6—KNIGHTS TEMPLAR

"During the Crusades…you do know about the Crusades, right?"

Sam gave him a blank stare.

Eli shook his head in disgust. "Robin Hood, surely you heard about him?"

Sam perked up in his seat, excited to finally know something. "I saw a cartoon once where Robin Hood was a fox. His friend Little John was a big bear, and they went around stealing money from the rich and giving it to the poor. It was pretty funny how they pulled tricks on Prince John and the Sheriff of Nottingham."

Eli's lips pressed thin. "A cartoon isn't exactly what I had in mind, but it might work. Remember how Prince John wanted to be the king instead of his brother, King Richard?"

"Yes, and John kept sucking his thumb when things didn't go his way."

Eli gave him a funny look. "Where was King Richard?"

"Hey, I think I do remember. He was fighting the Crusades." His tone sounded more like a question than a statement.

"The Crusades were no cartoon. Many people died on both sides, and there's nothing funny about that."

Sam's grin faded.

"The Crusades were wars brought about by arrogant Christians trying to push their beliefs on Muslims. That never works, by the way. After the Christians gained access to the holy places in and near Jerusalem, settlers started moving into these areas, but they were always being attacked. I received the task of protecting these people, while secretly securing holy artifacts. It was a big job, so I put together some good men and trained them to fight like no other soldiers. Our headquarters were in Solomon's temple, so everyone called us the Knights Templar.

"Over time, the tasks mainly consisted of keeping the artifacts secure and out of evil men's hands. The artifacts have great supernatural powers, and when used for evil, they could be devastating. Back then, I was called Hugues de Payens, the Grand Master of the Knights Templar. Technically, I still am since the appointment is for life, and I'm not dead. After eighteen years of leading the Templars, people started noticing I wasn't aging. I received a new task, so I faked my death and left. The Templars carried on without me, but eventually, greedy men betrayed them. The evil men disbanded the Templars and took all their assets, including the artifacts. Not long ago, I got the task to recover one. Did those nuns teach you about Hitler?"

"No, but I know about him from movies. He killed lots of people." Sam felt pride he knew another fact, but Hitler wasn't anything to smile about, so he curbed his enthusiasm.

"Hitler had acquired one of the artifacts called the Lance of Longinus, which made his armies invincible. I died three times getting my lance back from those stinking Nazis. His evil empire started to crumble shortly after."

"Your lance?"

"Yes, my lance. I've had many names, but my first was Longinus. You're the beginning of a new generation of the

Knights Templar, who will gather up and protect these artifacts."

"So, you only rescued me because I'm going to be a Knights Templar Granddaddy?"

"Grand Master. I rescued you because God gave me a vision to fulfill. What he does with you is His business. All I can do is complete the tasks."

Eli's gruff reply didn't make Sam feel any better. "Would you take me back to the sisters if I wanted?"

Eli swerved again when he looked into the mirror, but this time there wasn't a car to honk. "Why would you want to go back there?"

"I might get adopted by someone who wants me for me and not because of my birthmark."

Eli paused for a moment. "Sam, I think I misunderstood your question," he said softly. "God put us together, but I would want you whether you had a cross in your eye or not. If you lost all your powers today, I would still want you. I dropped a whole lot of information on you, and I'm sorry. Yes, I'll take you back to the group home if you want."

Abby nuzzled him. "I'll go wherever you decide."

Eli's words made Sam's heart warm. "No, I'll go with you. If you choose me, I choose you."

Eli grinned wide. "You do realize I'm going to be tough on you. I'm going to make you into the greatest warrior who has ever lived."

Sam had to admit that sounded pretty cool, but he had other pressing matters. "Can you do me a favor?"

"What?"

"Can you stop somewhere soon? I need to go to the bathroom."

Eli chuckled, nodding his head. "I need gas anyway."

Sam was squirming in his seat when Eli finally found a gas station. Just as soon as Eli parked and unlocked his door, Sam bolted for the convenience store. Thankfully, the bathroom was empty.

When he exited the bathroom, he noticed an angel and a demon standing by a man in a black hoodie. He wandered closer, acting as if he were picking out a candy bar.

The demon had a nasty grin that set Sam on edge. "Go on, Jerry, pull out your gun. You can't rob a place if you don't pull out your gun."

The angel pleaded to the man. "You'll get caught or worse, killed. How will you feed your family then? Swallow your pride and ask for help. Your dad will help you."

The demon smirked at the angel, as if he'd already won. "You don't need anybody's stinking help. Your stingy dad still has the first dime he ever had. Be a man and get the money yourself. Pull out your gun, and they'll start throwing cash at you."

"What would Jennifer think of you doing this? Do you want Ricky growing up without a dad?" The angel's words fell off the man like rain on an umbrella.

"No bigger shame than letting your family starve. Isn't this the store that turned you down for a job? That guy behind the register is probably the one who took *your* job. He deserves to be robbed, and if he pulls out a gun, shoot him."

The man started to reach into his bulging pocket.

Sam's chest burned from anger, and he couldn't help stepping closer to the man. "Hey, Jerry."

The startled man whirled around, but thankfully, he hadn't pulled out his gun.

"I know I'm just a kid, but I got a message for you. Jennifer and Ricky need you. I wish every day *my* dad was around." Sam pointed to the camera up by the ceiling. "If you do what you're thinking, you'll go to jail."

The man's eyes went wide, and his jaw dropped as he decided to flee. Unfortunately for him, he ran smack dab into Eli's rock-hard chest.

Eli instinctively grabbed the man's hood, exposing his frightened face. "Is there a problem?"

"Eli, this man's wife and son are hungry and he has no money. He wants to sell the gun he has in his pocket and wondered if you might be interested."

"Is that so?" Eli lifted the hood so much the man's feet were about to leave the ground. "How much do you think the gun is worth?"

Sam creased his brow before answering. "A fair price as long as he calls his dad first. But no matter what, he doesn't leave here with the gun."

Eli grinned at Sam. "I can tell you're going to make life interesting." He took the would-be robber out of the store like a man holding a puppet on a string.

The demon glared at Sam. "Where did the brat come from? I almost had him convinced."

The angel shook his head, looking at the camera. "Not sure, but I like him. I just wish I'd thought of the camera angle."

The demon leaned closer to Sam. "I think I'll start in on him for messing up my plans."

The angel grinned. "He might be more than you can handle. He seems different from the rest."

Sam hadn't made eye contact with either one, until he jerked his eyes up to glare at the demon. "I think *I'll* start in on *you*, and I *will* if you don't stop bothering Jerry."

If a demon could be scared, Sam just did it. The demon backed right through the candy section, staring in shock as Sam's eyes followed him as he went. He continued backing until he went right through the wall and out of the store. Sam smiled at the angel. "I hope I helped."

The angel smiled back. "You *can* see me. You can't imagine how much you helped. I almost lost Jerry, and now you've given me so much to work with. I should strike while the iron's hot. Thanks." Halfway through the front wall he turned back. "What's your name, kid?"

"Sam," he replied, grinning.

"I'm guessing we'll be hearing more about you." The angel winked and disappeared through the wall.

Eli came back into the store without Jerry. "You do realize you look like you're talking to yourself. You're making the guy at the counter nervous."

Sam glanced at the salesclerk. "Better to be nervous than shot."

Eli chuckled. "Good point. Now, are you going to get some candy or not? I'm ready to pay for our gas."

Sam grinned and grabbed a Baby Ruth. On occasion, Sister Gertrude had taken him for a walk outside the group home. Every time, she had allowed him to pick out a candy bar at the convenience store. He suspected she only took him so she could get her own supply, since she would always leave with about a dozen, but he didn't mind. He liked the candy, but pretending to be free was what he liked most.

Once they were back in the truck, Eli gave Abby the beef jerky he'd bought for her. "I'm guessing you stopped him from robbing the place?" Eli put the truck in drive and headed out to the road.

Sam shoved the last of his Baby Ruth into his mouth so he couldn't speak.

"What's the hurry?" Eli frowned at him through the mirror.

"Sworry," he mumbled through his full mouth. Sister Gertrude always made him rush so the other orphans wouldn't get jealous. He finally swallowed. "Yeah, Jerry had a demon trying to get him to rob the place. Did you get his gun?"

"It's in the glove box. I also made sure he called his dad. From the sound of the conversation, I think everything will be OK for him."

"Good," said Sam, smiling. "It's pretty lucky we stopped, or he'd be going to jail."

Eli chuckled. "Luck has nothing to do with it."

"But we only stopped because I had to go to the bathroom."

"That's how it works. Why didn't you run when you figured out what was happening?"

Sam shrugged his shoulders.

"Did you even think about leaving?"

Sam thought back and shook his head. "The demon made me mad. When the angel talked about his wife and son, I knew I had to do something."

"Exactly, because it was the right thing to do. You didn't know him, and you knew he had a gun. Most other people would've run, but you tried to save him from a terrible mistake. You not only saved him, you saved his family from a lot of pain. You have the heart of a Templar."

Eli's praise made Sam uncomfortable. "To tell you the truth, I was plenty scared. I'm glad I went to the bathroom first."

Eli chuckled. "Courage is doing the right thing in the face of fear. Since the danger has passed, how do you feel?"

Sam thought for a moment and then smiled. "Pretty good."

"That's what it's all about. Try to hold on to that feeling because I'm about to put you through some tough training. Did you enjoy your candy bar?" Eli started opening his Snickers.

"Yeah." For a fleeting moment, he wondered if Eli would give him his candy bar, but he was sadly mistaken.

"I'm glad you did because you won't be getting another any time soon. Knights in training don't eat junk." Eli took a small bite and closed his eyes in satisfaction. "For something so bad for you, these things are so delicious."

Eli took fifteen minutes to eat his Snickers. When he finally wadded up the wrapper, Sam wished he hadn't rushed eating his Baby Ruth.

"There's a blanket and pillow under your seat. Make yourself comfortable. I'm driving through the night. When you wake up, we'll be home and training begins." Eli's smirk wasn't comforting. "You're going to need all the rest you can get."

7—I DIDN'T SIGN UP FOR THIS

Sam gasped at the sensation of falling. He reached out to break his fall, but something had him trapped. His momentary fright dwindled when he landed on the warm leather seat he had, only moments ago, been sleeping on. Tangled in his blanket, he squirmed around until he managed to stick his head out like a turtle coming out of its shell. Gently, he moved Abby over so he could free himself and sit up. Once he looked through the windshield, he figured out why he was off balance. The pickup climbed a steep incline on a rough dirt road, if you could call the overgrown path a road. It was nothing like the paved road they had just left. The grass, bushes, and saplings were trying very hard to cover up the two parallel paths. The haze in the air gave the appearance of morning, but the mountain hid the sun.

"I thought that might wake you up." Eli's roguish grin disappeared from the mirror as the pickup lurched into a hole and then violently bounced back. "The shortcut to the cabin is bumpy, but I need to take it once in a while so the path doesn't grow over. You never know when you might need to make a quick getaway."

Sam rubbed his eyes and inspected the road again as Eli drove over a small tree. "I think you might be losing the battle."

Eli smirked. "That's exactly what I've been thinking."

Abby pawed at her eyes and then yawned. "Did you have to take the shortcut? That was the best sleep I've had in about a year."

"Sorry, Abs. I'm anxious to get home and this is the fastest way. Besides, Sam needed to see the shortcut."

After ten more minutes of bouncing all over the cab, the pickup finally leveled out to the backside of the cabin. Eli wheeled the pickup around the side. A small stack of firewood leaned against the west wall.

"So cool, you have a fireplace. That's much better than the useless radiators we had at the group home."

"I'm glad you approve." Eli grinned wide as he parked the truck in the drive.

Abby nudged Sam with her nose. "Hey, I think you're digging your own grave."

"What?" He scratched her behind the ears.

"I think you're about to find out." Abby opened the door with her mouth and jumped out, followed closely by Sam.

The cabin had timber at the back, but the front was wide-open. The clearing had rocky patches of dirt with a few grass clumps and several old tree stumps. Although they were on top of a mountain, much taller ones surrounded them. He couldn't deny the beauty of the lush trees and wildflowers, but Sam had business that was more important. Eli exited the truck and began stretching from the long drive. Sam jogged awkwardly toward the cabin.

Eli yelled after him. "Hey, where's the fire?"

Sam continued because his situation was serious. "Bathroom."

"You won't find one in there."

Abby giggled, and Sam carefully stopped. "Then where?"

"You can pee behind any tree."

Sam didn't have time for this. He shook his head and clutched his cramping stomach.

Eli opened his pickup door and came out holding a roll of toilet paper. "We don't have a bathroom, but we do have an outhouse." He pointed at a little building about the size of a small closet that sat thirty yards to the left of the cabin. "You'll need this. I took the only roll when I left."

Sam carefully walked back, grabbed the roll, and headed for the outhouse as fast as he could go, which wasn't very fast in his current predicament.

"Be sparing with the paper. If we run out, we have to use leaves."

***

When Sam finally escaped the foul-smelling outhouse, he found Eli sitting on a stump with an axe on his lap.

Eli's eyes showed the smile his mouth hinted at. "Everything OK?"

Sam's face felt hot from embarrassment. "Yeah, not use to traveling, I guess."

Eli surveyed the massive pile of wood to his side. "I split all this wood for winter. It comes in handy for the wood to be close to the cabin. What do you think we should do about that?"

Sam looked at the wood, the stack next to the cabin, and then Eli. "I'm guessing *we* should stack the firewood by the cabin."

Eli stood up and brought the axe down on the stump in one quick but powerful strike, leaving the handle sticking up in the air. "I already did my part by splitting it. Now, do yours by stacking it. I'm going to take a nap."

"But what about the pictures of my parents?"

Eli gestured to the east. "Do you see the sun there?"

Past the misty valley to another mountain, the sun started to break over the trees. Sam stood in awe for moment until Eli's throat clearing caught his attention. "Yeah."

"Daylight is for training. Nighttime is for talking and looking at pictures."

Sam thought about asking how stacking wood was supposed to help him become a mighty knight but decided it wasn't worth complaining about. Instead, he bent over, picked up two sticks of split wood, and headed to the cabin. After he stacked the first load, he turned to find Eli hadn't moved, except for crossing his arms. He trudged back to the pile. "This would be a lot faster if we used your pickup."

"Like I said, I'm going to take a nap, and you're too young to drive."

Sam bent over and picked up two more sticks. He opened his mouth to complain, but Eli's glare stopped him short. After a few more trips, he noticed Eli had moved to the porch. He sat in an old rocker with his feet up on the railing, eyes closed.

Abby sat on the stump next to the axe and watched him work.

***

The sun was high in the sky when he stacked the last two pieces of wood. For the first time in his life, he was soaked in sweat. He had blisters and splinters, and he had even stubbed his toe, but he couldn't help smiling when he stepped back and admired the huge stack of wood by the cabin.

A window opened several feet above the stack, and Eli stuck his head out. "Just in time for lunch. Come around to the porch."

In the short time he'd stood admiring his work, his body had grown stiff, but he pushed through it for food. On the porch, Eli had a sandwich and a large glass of water. Sam was hungry, but his thirst was desperate. He drained the glass in one try.

Eli took the empty glass and handed him the plate. "Training made you thirsty." He gestured to one of two chairs around a small table. The table had a checkerboard design for the top, but no checkers. "Sit here and I'll get you another glass of water."

Abby polished off her roast beef sandwich, and Sam was about halfway through his when Eli returned. He quickly took the glass and downed the water before digging into the rest of his sandwich. Eli took the chair Abby had left. In no time at all, he stuck the last bite into his mouth.

"Hard work makes food taste better, huh?" Eli grinned.

Sam leaned back in his chair and took a deep breath of satisfaction. "It was good, thanks."

"The water tasted pretty good too, didn't it?"

"Can I get some more?"

Eli looked to his left and then to his right. "I don't have a demon following me around, do I?"

Sam suspected Eli already knew the answer. "No."

"Good. You had me worried. For a second there, I thought you were reading my mind."

"Huh?"

Eli chuckled. "You can get more water."

Eli talked nonsense, but Sam was too tired to care. He got up and grabbed his glass.

"You're going to need something bigger than that."

Sam stopped and would have narrowed his eyes, but he was too tired to put out the effort.

Eli pointed to the right of the cabin. "Over there is a cistern."

A huge tin barrel on a metal stand was next to the cabin. Sam walked over to the edge of the porch and leaned out over the railing. The barrel had a domed top with a pipe running from the cabin's gutters.

"Do you know what a cistern is?"

"No." Sam had a bad feeling the barrel had something to do with more work.

"The cistern holds all our water. We haven't had much rain this spring. Usually, it's running over this time of year, but danged if you didn't drink the last of our water supply. We need to fill the cistern."

Sam put the empty glass down on the table.

Eli energetically negotiated the seven porch steps. Sam missed them before, but two metal buckets sat at the bottom of the steps.

"Come on and I'll show you what needs to be done." Eli picked up the two buckets and headed for the cistern.

Sam followed, but not enthusiastically. Every muscle he had screamed in protest. He didn't know it was even possible, but he limped on both legs simultaneously. Eli grinned as Sam hobbled over to him.

"Don't worry, you'll loosen up after a couple of trips." Eli pointed to the valley. "There's a spring at the bottom of that path. When you fill your buckets, bring them back and pour them into this bigger bucket." The rope tied to the bigger bucket looped around a pulley that hung above the cistern.

"After that, pull on this rope until the bucket catches and dumps into the cistern like so." Eli quickly pulled the empty bucket up until the top of the bucket hit a wooden lever. A semicircular arm pushed the bottom of the bucket out while another arm pushed the top in, making the bucket tip over the top of the cistern. "I'll move the lid before you get back. Once you dump the water, jerk on the rope to release the bucket." Again, Eli showed what he meant. "Daylight's burning."

Sam's tight back painfully stretched when he grabbed the metal bucket handles. His stiff fingers ached as he lifted them up and headed down the path.

"The water's good, but don't drink too much while you're down there. You'll get sick."

Sam didn't reply. The path was steep but clear of brush, so the walking was easy. He started to hear the water, and after rounding the bend, the spring came into view. The water came out of the side of the mountain about ten feet above a pool. Any normal day he would have appreciated the beauty, but today he was tired and angry.

Abby sat by the waterfall. "Eli fills the buckets from here."

Before filling his buckets, he set them down and stuck his head into the falling water. His breath caught, but the cold water was refreshing. He turned his head sideways and began catching some in his mouth.

"Not too much. Remember what Eli said."

Her warning was the final straw. In defiance, he continued drinking until he couldn't hold any more.

"You're going to regret that."

"I was thirsty." He filled both buckets, avoiding her eyes.

The climb didn't go nearly as fast as the descent. He hadn't gone far before noticing the water sloshing uncomfortably in his stomach. He stopped to rest at the bend. Abby didn't say a word while he caught his breath. During the next fifty yards, the sloshing in his stomach turned to churning, causing him to pause. He wished he hadn't drunk so much. Once he had the nausea under control, he took off again. The churning started again after only a few yards. He started to heave. Dropping the buckets, he fell to his knees and began throwing up. He lost everything in his stomach, including his lunch. To Abby's credit, she never said a word.

He had to rest seven more times before he made it to the cistern. When he left the spring, the buckets were brim full. He knew some had splashed out on his return trip, but losing half hit him hard. *I'll have to make twice as many trips at this rate.* He poured the remaining water into the bigger bucket and pulled on the rope. His tired arms strained to raise the bucket high enough to trigger the release. With one last pull, the bucket dumped into the cistern. He jerked on the rope, releasing the bucket.

Eli stood on the porch, smiling, holding a mug. "I was beginning to think you were lost. At least now I have enough water to make coffee."

Sam clenched his jaw. Not only was Eli saying he was slow, he planned to *use* some of the costly water. Sam grabbed the buckets and angrily headed back down to the spring. *At least he didn't ask if I got sick.*

"I think he already knows," said Abby, following along.

"Did you tell him?" He gave her an accusing stare.

"No, but you did take a while coming back, and you still have some vomit on your shirt."

"I don't want you telling him what I'm thinking." He wasn't particularly mad at Abby, but she happened to be convenient.

"OK, I won't." Abby's tone was annoyingly cheery.

"You'd think a two-thousand-year-old man could figure out a way to have water without carrying it up a mountain."

"I think he has."

Sam wrinkled his forehead. "What did he do before me?"

"Let's just say this isn't about having water. He's trying to get you in shape. To be honest, you're kind of soft."

She has a good point. He already had done more exercise today than the sum total of his entire life. Sam rounded the bend.

Abby loped to the spring. "Thank you."

"For what?"

"You said I had a good point."

"If I don't talk to you directly, can you at least pretend you don't hear me?"

"Sure."

"Was Eli trying to be funny about making coffee?" He stepped up to fill the buckets.

"I'm not sure. Eli loves his coffee."

With both buckets full, he began the long march back up the hill. "If I say mean things in my head, ignore them," he said through gritted teeth.

Abby chuckled.

***

Sam struggled to pull up his fifteenth bucket to dump in the cistern. His arms were useless so he wrapped the rope around his waist and began backing up. Slowly but surely, the bucket rose, tripped, and tipped. He gave the line a jerk, and the bucket released. He wavered a moment, seriously thinking about collapsing. Instead, he took a deep breath and picked up the two buckets for another trip to the spring.

"Hey." Eli stood on the porch, pointing to the mountain to the left of the cabin.

Sam couldn't think straight. "What?"

"Do you see the sun?"

"No."

"Exactly. The sun is below the tree line. It's time to come in and eat. After that, I'll show you some pictures of your folks."

Sam hurt from his toenails to the hair on his head, but nothing would stop him from hearing about his parents. He started to run for the porch and almost fell. Wisely, he decided to slow down. *I wonder if I look like them.*

8—MIGHTY SUSPICIOUS

The inside of the cabin was simple enough. To the left was the kitchen, straight ahead a plain wooden table with four chairs, and a sitting area to the right. The comfortable-looking couch and recliner faced the fireplace, but what made Sam's heart leap for joy was the huge TV on the mantle. "We have electricity?"

"Of course we have electricity," said Eli, attending to something sizzling on the stove. "It's not the dark ages. Believe me, I would know. I lived through them."

Abby put her front paws on the cabinet by the stove, sniffing toward the smoking pot. "Mmmm, I love bacon."

Sam's stomach growled in agreement. "I thought since we didn't have a bathroom, and there were no electric polls, we probably didn't have any." Sam glanced around to realize there were lights on in the kitchen and above the table. This was good news.

Eli chuckled as he opened the refrigerator door and grabbed a container of butter. "We've got a bathroom. The stool's just not hooked up yet." He pointed to the back of the cabin. "I've only been here thirty years. I'll finish the plumbing soon enough, now that I have some good help."

He winked at Sam while stirring the pot with a wooden spoon.

"Where's the electricity coming from?"

"I put solar panels on top of the mountain to the west. They charge up the batteries under the floor. If they run down, which they haven't yet, we can turn on the generator down at the shed. So, like the water, use all you need, but don't be wasteful."

Eli poured a can of green beans into the pot. Steam erupted, and the sizzling from the pan grew louder. "The bathroom's at the end of the hallway, my room is on the left, and my office is on the right. You're pretty ripe, so go take a shower. Dinner will be ready when you're out."

Sam paused. "Where are my clothes?"

"I figured your clothes from the group home wouldn't do out here, so I bought you some new ones before I left. I'm pretty sure they'll fit. They're in the bottom two drawers of the cabinet in the bathroom. Just leave your dirty clothes in a pile on the floor.

***

The hot shower soothed his aching muscles, but he didn't waste any time. There was a price to be paid for every drop that went down the drain. He quickly soaped up, rinsed, and turned off the water within a couple of minutes.

Sam opened the first drawer, but everything inside blurred together. His eyes adjusted to the varying shades of green and brown to realize this drawer contained camouflage-colored underwear, T-shirts, and socks. He chuckled as he put them on. The second drawer had camo-colored jeans and long-sleeve shirts. He put on the jeans, but the shirt was too hot for summer. The smell of dinner coming through the door made his mouth water.

As promised, Eli had dinner ready. He sat at the table, grinning, as Sam walked in. "How do you like your new clothes?"

Sam froze in place. "Can you see me now?"

Eli and Abby laughed.

Eli looked around in an exaggerated way. "Abby, where did he go?"

"I don't know. He just disappeared."

Sam burst out laughing. "Thanks, these are pretty cool."

"And handy. Out here, it's better to see than to be seen. Well, don't be shy. Let's eat."

Sam took the seat next to the empty plate, which was across from Eli and to the right of Abby, who also sat at the table. His stomach growled at the sight of food. He recognized the green beans in the pot next to his plate, but not the food in the pan.

"You're going to like my famous goulash. Trust me." Eli reached over and loaded Sam's plate with a generous helping. He also filled Abby's plate, saving his own for last. "Take some green beans and pass them on. We don't have all night."

He dished out some green beans with bits of bacon and onions mixed in. They smelled delicious. When he passed the pot over to Abby, she tilted her head sideways in a funny way.

"If you don't mind." Abby raised a paw for emphasis.

He laughed and dished her out some before putting the pot within Eli's reach.

"Thanks." Abby leaned into her plate and sniffed.

Eli sawed off three pieces of bread from a loaf, spread butter on them, and tossed one onto each of Sam's and Abby's plates.

Sam scooped up a forkful of goulash when he noticed Abby and Eli staring at him.

Eli raised one eyebrow. "Grace?"

Sam awkwardly put his fork down. Abby had her head bowed, so he did the same.

"God, thank you for the food you put before us, the strength to do what is right, and the faith not to question your will. Amen. Now dig in."

There wasn't much talking as they devoured the tasty food. Sam couldn't think of when he had better. After two helpings of everything, he decided he better quit before he got sick. His exhaustion and full stomach were making his eyelids droop.

Eli and Abby were staring at him. "What?" he asked drowsily.

"As soon as you wash the dishes and clean up the kitchen, I'll show you some pictures."

Sam's eyes popped wide open as he jumped up to start clearing the table.

"I'd help, but no hands." Abby didn't sound too sincere.

Sam gave her a little smirk. "That excuse will get old. You open doors pretty easily."

She brought her plate to him using her mouth. "Here you go."

Sam grinned, taking the plate. "Hey, you pretty much cleaned yours. Maybe we should let you lick them all clean."

"Yuck, and get your germs? No thanks."

"Let's stick to soap and water," said Eli, walking to the back of the cabin. "I'm going to dig up those pictures."

***

Fifteen minutes later, Sam stared at the folder Eli laid on the clean table.

"I don't have many. I printed these from the news articles after the crash. I say crash, but there's no proof of one besides you." Eli pushed the folder across the table.

Sam almost ripped the folder in his rush to open it. Inside were three pictures. The first picture was of a good-looking man, smiling and waving. Sam didn't think the business suit matched the tan, rugged face.

Eli gestured toward the picture. "That's your dad, David. Do you remember him?"

Sam shook his head as he set the picture to the side. The next picture also showed his dad waving, but next to him stood a beautiful redheaded woman. "That's my mom!"

"Yes, do you remember her?"

"I think I do. I'm not sure." He stared unblinkingly at her face. "She's really pretty, isn't she?"

"Yes, she is," agreed Eli.

Sam set the picture aside to look at the third and last photo. Eli leaned forward. He thought for a second Eli had something to say, but he only gestured encouragingly. The last picture contained a group of people. His eyes immediately found his mom and dad, but then he shuddered. He ripped the picture in half. He threw one piece away like trash, but clung to the other.

Eli picked up the piece Sam had thrown to the table. "Why did you rip the picture apart?"

"It has demons in it."

Sam stared at his piece of the torn picture for a quite a while. His mother had him pinned to the front of her legs with her palm. He could almost feel her warm hand on his chest, his heart. She was so beautiful. He had to blink back tears. He set the torn picture down and went back to the second picture.

"How many people are in this picture?" Eli turned his piece of the torn picture toward Sam.

He didn't need to look up. "There are three demons standing by the tall man, and the ugly man is possessed. The demon is sticking its head out a little." A terrible thought occurred to Sam, glancing up. "I'm not related to them, am I?"

"No, not at all," Eli replied quickly.

"Good." Sam breathed a sigh of relief. "Those two are rotten."

"Why do you say that?"

"No angels."

Eli's frown creased his forehead. "I don't understand."

"It means those two only listen to demons. The angels gave up on them. The ugly man isn't even thinking for himself since he let the demon inside, and the other guy has three demons. I've never seen that before, but it can't be good." Sam went back to his pictures, but he could tell Eli was forcing himself to be patient by the way he was fidgeting. "What's my mother's name?"

"Sarah Parker Golden."

"Golden?"

"Yes, Parker was her maiden name."

"Oh." Sam frowned. "She had me before she married my father?"

"No, no, nothing like that. Your real name is Samuel Parker Golden." Before Sam could ask why, Eli continued. "I didn't give the sisters your full name because you were kind of famous at the time. I didn't want to put you in danger."

Sam creased his brow. "Danger?"

Eli pointed at the tall man in the picture. "That's Seth Abbadon Tanas, and the ugly one is his henchman, Lamia. That picture was taken right after a US Senate debate. David, your dad, ran against him for the US Senate seat for Missouri. He handily defeated Tanas in that debate." Eli glanced at the picture. "Tanas isn't happy, but what about the demons?"

Sam hesitated to lean in. These demons were different from all the others he had faced. They were less like humans and more like monsters. "No, they're not happy at all."

Eli nodded. "I bet they're not. Your dad was set to win the election, but that very night he disappeared and I saved you. Mighty suspicious circumstances, if you ask me. After I dropped you off at the group home, I went back and started to search for your folks. The next day, the whole country helped me search. Not a trace was found of your family or the airplane. I don't know what happened to them."

"But you said *I* was in danger."

"I suspected Tanas had something to do with the plane crash, and now that I know demons were involved, I'm sure he did. With your dad out of the way, he kept his Senate seat. A month after your family went missing, they stopped searching. The government didn't want to spend any more money on what seemed like a lost cause. Tanas made headlines when he paid out of his own pocket for the search to continue. He looked like a hero, but I bet he only wanted to confirm your deaths. Not to mention the national publicity he got. I mean, think of it. The man who's about to beat you in an election disappears, and you spend upward of a million dollars trying to find him. The press loved it."

"You think Tanas killed my parents?" Sam grabbed the torn picture out of Eli's hand.

"Not personally, but I think he was behind it."

As Sam stared at the picture, a deep burning sensation started in his heart and began to expand. He took turns staring at Tanas and then his parents. *He's the reason I lost my parents. He's the reason I'm alone.*

Abby nudged Sam's leg. "Sam, you're not alone."

Eli glanced at Abby and then grabbed Tanas's picture from Sam. "Guard your heart, boy. Hate will ruin you. You have powerful gifts. Your gifts will help you overcome evil such as Tanas, but they won't work if your heart is full of hate."

Sam tried to grab the picture back, but Eli was too quick. He'd never felt anything so intense. He desperately tried again, lunging forward.

Eli stood up with such force his chair slid back several feet, hit a rough place in the wood floor and then crashed over backward. "Boy!"

Sam gasped in shock to see not the man who had adopted him, but a warrior to be feared.

"Calm yourself," Eli said softly, but with menace.

The overwhelming anger he had only moments ago drained from him. His hands trembled weakly, and he didn't know why.

Eli slowly retrieved his chair, his gaze never leaving Sam's face. "You just had your first experience with hate." His voice was even as he gently put the picture of Tanas on the table. "If you let hate have control, you'll be no better than him." He gestured toward the picture. "Do you know the difference between justice and revenge?"

Sam slowly shook his head.

"It's the difference between life and death." Eli picked up all the pictures and put them into the folder. "I'll give you the pictures again when you can tell me what I mean. I put a blanket and pillow by the couch. You can sleep there until I make better arrangements."

Sam made his way to the couch and collapsed. Exhaustion set in, but he managed to open his eyes enough to catch a glimpse of Eli covering him with the blanket.

Abby jumped up beside him. "Sweet dreams."

9—JUSTICE OR REVENGE

Morning came way too early for Sam. He assumed the loud banging of pots and pans in the kitchen was Eli preparing breakfast. The smell of coffee brewing confirmed his suspicions. Abby jostled him when she jumped down, and he muffled a whimper of pain from his sore muscles.

"Sleep much longer and you'll miss breakfast." Eli's voice was much too cheerful this early in the morning.

The aroma of bacon tempted him to move as he debated the merits of sleep versus hunger.

"Eli's not kidding. You better get up and eat. You're going to need the energy."

Sam painfully swung his feet over the side of the couch and sat up, eyes still shut.

"Being it's your first morning, I'm going to cut you some slack. You have one minute to fold your blanket, wash your face, and sit down at the table. Tomorrow, I expect you to get up and help me cook."

Sam decided eating was overrated. He fell back over into the couch and covered himself with the blanket. He expected to get yelled at, but when nothing happened, he started to relax. The sounds of Eli and Abby eating floated lazily through his mind as he drifted back to sleep.

A bolt of lightning couldn't have shocked Sam's body more than the bucket of ice-cold water Eli had thrown on him. Water he had toiled to bring up the mountain. He instantly stood, dripping wet, and stared at Eli's grinning face.

"Put your boots on and come outside. Be quick, unless you want me to waste another bucket on you." Eli pointed down at a pair of leather lace-up work boots sitting beside the couch.

Sam shivered from the cold water, but he didn't hesitate this time to follow Eli's command. When he opened the front door, he half expected another bucket. He worried the couple of minutes it took to lace up his new boots would be too long. However, Eli wasn't holding a bucket. He held what looked like the head of a spear.

"Today, we have sword practice."

Sam forgot all about his sore muscles as he reached out his hand. "Sweet, but isn't that kind of small for a sword?"

Eli drew back so Sam couldn't reach. "This weapon has been known as the Lance of Longinus, the Spear of Destiny, and the Holy Lance. Those names are too long for my taste, so I call her BK." Eli turned the lance upside down to show the round metal band at the bottom. "This is where you would attach a shaft. Over the centuries, I discovered BK has some remarkable properties." He pointed the tip down and loudly said, "Sword."

The tip started to extend, growing in size until the weapon had transformed into a massive double-edged sword. "I wanted to give you the history of this weapon over breakfast, but the sun's well up, and daylight is for training." With the point sticking into the wooden porch, he balanced the sword by the handle. "For all my many years, BK has only changed shape for me. Now, let's see whether you truly are my replacement."

The sword stood head high to Sam. He stepped up and grabbed the leather handle as Eli let go. For a second, Sam thought the sword was going through the floor, but then he realized it was shrinking.

"It changes shape based on what I need at the time." Eli grinned. "And now, BK does the same for you. It's extremely sharp, so be careful." Eli stepped back.

Sam lifted BK and took a couple of practice swings. The leather grip molded to his hands. "It's light."

"As you grow and become stronger, BK will grow with you. Now follow me." Eli traversed the steps and walked around the west side of the cabin between the wood stack and outhouse.

Sam followed, swiping the sword and pretending to be a pirate. He was prepared for another long day of work, but this would be fun. Eli finally stopped where the shortcut began. Sam looked down the steep grade where the pickup had climbed yesterday. He could barely make out the path for the small trees, brush, and bushes.

Eli pointed to a small tree in the middle of the path. "Cut the sapling down as close to the ground as possible."

The sapling was about an inch thick at the base so Sam gripped the sword like a baseball bat, took aim, and swung hard. The momentum of his swing turned him around to face Eli. He sheepishly grinned.

Eli raised an eyebrow and pointed over Sam's shoulder. He figured Eli wanted him to try again. He turned back around and, as he thought, he had missed. Taking better aim, he raised the sword as the sapling toppled over.

"Like I said, sharp. You won't need to swing so hard for something that small."

"Whoa, I didn't think I hit it." Sam examined where he had cut the sapling in two.

"I think you have the idea now. I want you to clear the shortcut. You'll get tired, but you can never get sloppy. BK can lop off an arm or leg just as easily, not to mention a head." Eli smirked at Abby. "My warning is for you too."

"Don't worry. I won't let him cut off my head." Using her mouth, she dragged the sapling over to the side. "You cut, and I'll clear."

Sam grinned. "Nice, I get help today."

"I suppose you think Eli didn't work me the whole time I was here?"

Sam thoughtfully glanced at Eli who stood with his arms crossed. "No, I bet he *trained* you too."

"Talking is for when the sun goes down. Daylight is for *training*." Eli's grim face made Sam move as much as his words. After a couple of minutes, he glanced back to see Eli had left.

Although sword training was little more than hard work, he had fun for a while. BK easily cut through overhanging limbs, bushes, saplings, and occasionally, rocks that got in the way. At first, he swung the sword just for pleasure, but as he began to tire, Tanas crept into his mind. After that, with every swipe of the sword, he was cutting Tanas to pieces. He imagined an arm here, a leg there, across the stomach, and his favorite, Tanas's head toppling over like the sapling. He guessed he had gone about a hundred yards when his shoulders started aching badly enough that he needed to rest. Surprisingly, his legs hurt just as bad from trying to stay balanced on such a steep grade. He stuck BK in the ground and sat on the hillside. "What do you think BK stands for?"

"I thought you were never going to rest." Abby dragged off the bush he'd severed and then sat down next to him. "I don't know, maybe Black Knight."

"I'm thinking Beast Killer."

"How about Be Kind or I'll lop off your head?"

Sam laughed. "Sister Gertrude always said Bee's Knees for something good."

"Just ask Eli. I'm sure it's something manly."

He wanted to pet her, but his arms were too heavy to lift, so he leaned into her. Thirst plagued his throat, but the thought of climbing the hill to get a drink kept him from going. When his stomach growled, he realized it had been a while since he ate because he slept through breakfast.

"You should've eaten breakfast."

"Yeah, I know…I will tomorrow." He sat in silence for a moment, taking in the beauty of the mountain. The wildflowers speckled the landscape of shade and sun and were dazzling to the eye. "What do you think Eli means about justice and revenge?"

"I can't say."

"You don't know?"

"Eli made me promise not to tell you."

"How am I supposed to know if someone doesn't tell me?"

"Eli thinks you're smart enough to figure it out on your own. Any ideas?"

"He said it was the difference between life and death, so I'm guessing justice is life, and revenge is death." He turned to Abby, hoping she would either agree or disagree, but she didn't give a hint in either direction, so he continued. "I'm also guessing hate goes with revenge since he said hate would ruin me. Revenge is bad and justice is good."

"Think about how you felt when you found out Tanas killed your parents."

Sam's heart stung, and he clutched his chest.

"It makes you mad, right?"

"All I want to do is make him hurt. Make him hurt like I hurt."

"What if he were here? What would you do?"

"I'd take BK and cut off his head."

"What if he had a gun on you?"

"I wouldn't care. I'd still take BK and cut off his head."

"You answered Eli's question."

"Huh?" Sam looked at Abby in confusion. *How did I answer Eli's question?* He sat for a few moments, thinking about their conversation.

"I hear Eli coming."

They both jumped up and started to work again. A few minutes later, Sam heard him approaching.

"I brought you a drink." Eli poured water into a bowl for Abby and handed Sam the jug. "When the sun is straight up, I'll have lunch ready at the cabin. Bring the sword."

Sam took a long draw of water. Before handing the jug back, he took another.

"You can keep the jug, but bring it when you break for lunch." Eli started climbing back up the mountain.

"Eli," Sam said, trying to stop him. He coughed a little when some water went down his windpipe.

Eli turned without saying a word.

"I think I understand the difference between justice and revenge."

"Good for you, but nighttime is for talking. You can tell me your revelation after supper."

He took another drink as he watched Eli leave. He was pretty sure he'd figured out what Eli had meant, but now he had to wait all day to check. He put the water jug and Abby's bowl under some shade. "Is he always that way?"

"Yes," Abby said simply.

Abby's mouth had a few cuts from moving the brush. She looked as tired as he felt. Her black fur shined in the sun and looked hot. She wasn't complaining, so he didn't, either. He picked up BK and began swinging.

***

By the time the sun was finally straight up in the sky, Sam and Abby had covered at least twice the distance they had before Eli brought the water. Soaked in sweat for the second day in a row, he motioned Abby to follow him.

***

The table held two plates of food. Each had two bologna sandwiches with slices of tomato and mayonnaise, potato chips, and a dill pickle. "I'm guessing this plate is mine." Sam sat down in front of the plate with the tall glass of milk. The other plate had a bowl of milk so Abby could drink.

While they both ate furiously fast, Sam heard Eli making an awful racket inside the cabin. He wasn't sure what he was doing, but it involved a lot of yelling. When he popped the last bite into his mouth, Eli walked out the front door. He looked hot and irritated.

"How far did you get?"

Sam thought he might ask, so he had an answer waiting. "A little past the dip in the road by the boulder with a rock on top."

Eli's irritated face turned into a smile. "I'm impressed."

"Didn't think we'd get that far?"

"No, I'm impressed you took notice where you stopped and brought everything back as I told you. You're about a quarter done. Three more days like today, and you'll be finished."

The praise felt good, but not as good as the prospect of being done for the day. "We're done?"

"Done with sword practice. The rest of the day you'll be carrying water."

Determined not to show his disappointment, Sam smiled and nodded his head.

Eli narrowed his eyes. "Is that good news?"

"It's cooler work because of the shade. I can get a drink anytime I want, and this way, Abby can rest."

Abby turned her hound face toward Sam. "I can go as long as you can," she said in a hurt tone.

Sam didn't mean to insult her and quickly tried to backtrack. "That's not what I meant. I'm the one who needs to train, not you."

The corners of Eli's mouth turned slightly upward. "Yes, that's very true, but she won't be resting. I need her for the project I have in the cabin."

Sam raised his eyebrows.

"It's a surprise. With her help, I hope to finish before you can make twenty trips. You surely can do five more than yesterday, since you won't be foolish enough to drink too much, right?"

Sam's smile faded slightly as he nodded and got up. He had hoped Eli didn't know about him getting sick.

***

Although his arms and legs were jelly and the sun was nearly below the tree line, he decided to make one last trip for water. He had done much better today. He still lost some water along the way, but much less than yesterday. Sam smiled with pride as he poured in the water from his twenty-first trip.

"Did you make twenty?" Eli asked gruffly from the porch.

Sam lowered the big bucket after dumping the water in the cistern. "Yeah, I made twenty." He first thought about bragging about his twenty-first trip, but what if Eli added more tomorrow?

Eli chucked the rest of his coffee from his cup over the rail. "Time to clean up for supper."

***

It wasn't until after his quick shower and changing into fresh clothes that he spotted the difference in the bathroom. In the corner, where there had only been a hole before, was a shiny new stool. He smiled when he checked the bowl for water. *That must be the surprise he'd been working on.* He reached out to flush, but decided against wasting the water.

Sam wiped the smile off his face when he opened the bathroom door. *Two can play at this game.*

Eli grinned from ear-to-ear as Sam emerged from the bathroom, but Sam never let on anything was different.

"What's for supper?" he asked stoically, taking his seat.

Eli's grin turned sour. "You've got eyes, don't you?"

Eli's comment seemed to have more meaning than just referring to the food. Sam stifled a grin as he surveyed the different dishes on the table. "Meatloaf, mashed potatoes, and corn. Smells good." He smiled up at Eli.

Eli pursed his lips as if he wanted to say something, but instead bowed his head and said grace over the meal. Sam smirked when Eli added a request for patience in his prayer.

***

It wasn't until they had finished the meal and cleaned up the kitchen that Sam finally relented. "So, does the stool work?"

Eli got up and went to the coffeepot to pour a cup. Sam thought he might be smiling, but there was no proof of that when he returned to the table. "A stool that doesn't work wouldn't be much good."

"I suppose not, but I sure wasn't going to waste water checking."

Eli tried to hide his grin by taking a sip of coffee. "OK, what's your revelation on justice and revenge?"

Sam was glad Eli put this off. As he carried water, he had more time to think on the differences. "Justice is about giving someone what they deserve. Revenge is about giving someone what *you* think they deserve."

Eli scratched the stubble on his chin with his thumb and forefinger. "So, what's the difference?"

"If you're mad at someone, you might do something stupid to get back at them. That's where life and death comes in. You might get killed trying for revenge."

"How's that different than justice?"

"Justice is like when a cop arrests someone for doing something bad. They're not thinking about making them pay, only catching them."

"What does all that mean for you and Tanas?"

"It means if I want Tanas to pay, I can't go running off with BK to cut off his head. I need to be smart."

"Emotions are what you're talking about. You can't let emotions rule your actions. Hate will change how you think. Don't get me wrong. You don't have to like Tanas, but you can't allow your anger to cloud your judgment."

Sam nodded.

"I put the pictures of your parents under your pillow. Don't stay up too late. We have another big day tomorrow." Eli got up to leave.

Sam hoped his recent victory held out for his next question. "What does BK stand for?"

Eli chuckled without turning around. "Butt Kicker."

Sam grinned as he sprawled out on the couch. Abby tucked in next to him before he opened the folder. The torn picture of Tanas was missing, which made him glad. He only wanted to think of his family tonight. He drifted off to sleep holding his favorite picture to his chest. The one *he* was in with his parents.

10—FIRST KISS, REALLY?

Three months of continuous training hadn't made Sam a bit taller, but he noticed BK had grown with his strength. He was also getting so efficient at fetching water he could run up the hills with two full buckets without losing a drop. To reward himself, he decided to take a little unauthorized break. Eli wasn't big on breaks. "Daylight's for training" was Eli's favorite saying. Well, Sam had thought of some training he might do if given the chance. After all, he'd been dying to take a dip in the spring all summer long.

Seldom did Eli leave him unattended, and even when he did, there was always the threat he'd show up unannounced. Not to mention, Abby barely let him out of her sight. Today, right after lunch, Eli and Abby had decided to go to town for supplies. This was the first time they had left him alone for any length of time, and he wouldn't waste the chance.

He figured he had about two hours. He knew better than to shirk his duties, so he planned to take the swim after he topped off the cistern. He had an excuse ready and waiting. Once he finished carrying water, he thought he would train by teaching himself how to swim instead of sitting around.

When Eli's truck disappeared around the bend, Sam climbed the ladder to check the water level. Over the last three months, he got into the habit of marking the water line and counting the trips it took to fill the cistern. Ten trips, he calculated. Sam dropped to the ground, grabbed the buckets, and sprinted down the hill.

***

After dumping his ninth load, he paused for the first time. He smiled at how good he felt. He might have been soft when he first came to the mountain, but now he was strong. Eli had shown him how to gauge time using the movement of the sun. He figured he had about an hour before they returned.

Grabbing the buckets, he ran to the spring. He debated whether he should swim in his underwear or go commando. He was anxious about going naked in such an open space, but wet underwear would bleed through his pants. Eli never missed a thing.

Sam filled the two buckets before stripping down. He wanted to be ready if he heard Eli's truck coming up the mountain.

The cold water refreshed his hot skin as he waded out into the pool. He gasped with a mixture of surprise and a bit of fear when he stepped off an unseen ledge and was suddenly neck deep. Sam realized there was more to swimming than he had originally thought. Quickly backpedaling, his legs scraped a rock, causing him to fall backward and submerge into the icy water. Panic took over. Sam struggled, legs kicking, arms flailing, and gasping for air, but sucking in water instead. The water boiled as he tried to find the surface. His feet found solid ground, and he kicked, propelling himself upward until his head broke water. Sputtering and coughing, he expelled the water from his lungs to find he was only waist deep.

He stood for a moment, collecting his wits. He calmed his breathing and looked around, fearing someone had seen him. He listened for Eli's truck, but there was no sound. *Some great knight I am, scared of a little water.* He debated whether he should get out now and pretend it never happened, but he quickly realized he wouldn't forget. He remembered Eli saying he needed to face his fears.

Slowly, Sam used his feet to plot out a path along the edge of the pool. He planned to teach himself how to swim, but he didn't want the water too deep. Once he marked off a ten-foot path, he took a deep breath, lowered his head in the water, and pushed himself forward. After a couple attempts, he needed to turn around. He found that by putting his hands out in front and then fanning them when his momentum slowed, he could propel himself through the water. He carefully stayed on his ten-foot run, and after eight successful attempts, his confidence grew. On the ninth trip, he began kicking his feet, which allowed him to make the ten-foot run in one try. He repeated the feat on the tenth.

Sam looked across the pool. He figured the distance was about double what he'd practiced and the water much deeper, at least in the middle. Glaring at the far side like an enemy, he started to launch across the pool, but then a sound caught his attention. He cocked his head to the side and held his breath to listen. The familiar sound of Eli's truck floated across the valley. Eli would be at the cabin in about ten minutes. He had to make the decision to try or give up.

Taking a deep breath, he lowered his body and kicked off toward the middle of the pool. He surfaced in the middle and tried to stand, but he couldn't touch. Instead, he took another breath and kicked off using only water instead of the ground. He didn't go far, but it worked. He surfaced about five feet from the other side, and this time, he found the bottom. He grinned wide, but he didn't have time for celebration.

He launched back to the other side. Again, he surfaced in the middle of the pool, took a breath, dropped below the surface, and kicked off, expecting nothing but water to help him move forward. However, this time, his right foot tangled in what felt like a vine. He kicked again, but his foot wasn't coming free. He tried to resurface to get air, but he couldn't quite reach the top. His fear grew as he attempted to free his leg from a vine. His air was running out. He tugged a couple of times, hoping to loosen the vine's grip enough to reach the surface.

His face still fell a few inches short. Splashing wildly, he tried to pull himself up, but his strength faded. The trees and mountain shimmered peacefully through the water. *If only I were taller*, he thought before the darkness overtook him.

***

Peaceful silence shrouded his senses. Sam liked it here, wherever here was, until the muffled thump. The pressure in his ears ached when the thump struck again. The pressure pumped from inside him, trying to get out through his blocked ears. Another thump moved painfully from his heart to his head. His ears popped, and the sound of the waterfall came rushing in. His chest rose like a balloon expanding, once, twice, three times, until he thought his lungs would explode. The churning in his stomach made him gag.

Sam's fear-stricken eyes opened to find someone attached to his face, covering his mouth. He lurched sideways, stomach spasming and water expelling from his mouth. He barely missed vomiting into the girl's face. Repeatedly, he heaved water from his lungs and stomach. The contractions broke only for a fraction of a second, allowing him to gasp in small mouthfuls of air, but as the water left his body, larger breaths were possible. The wonderful air hurt his lungs. Slowly, the coughs turned into deep breaths as his panic left him. He raised his head to thank the girl, but she was gone. Abby sat next to him, soaking wet, with her hound smile.

"Where'd the girl go?" Sam said hoarsely, clutching his chest in pain.

Abby tilted her head sideways. "Girl?"

He nodded. "The girl who saved me."

"There's no girl."

Sam frowned, trying to recall what he had seen. Could he have imagined the girl? He rolled to his knees and realized he was naked. "Don't look," he said quickly. When Abby turned her head, he got up, wobbled a little, and grabbed his underwear off the branch he had hung them on. "I woke up to a girl kissing me."

"I sensed you were in trouble so I jumped out of Eli's truck and came here to find you drowning. I dove in, pulled you free from the tree root and then dragged you here. You were pretty much a goner, so you probably imagined a girl. I mean, why would a girl be kissing you when you were almost dead?"

Sam finished putting on the rest of his clothes. "She wasn't actually kissing me. Remember when Eli showed me how to do CPR? Pump their chest a few times, grab their nose, and breathe into their mouth?"

"Sorry to disappoint you, but it was just me. I bounced a couple times on your chest, and you started to throw up."

All his life people told him he wasn't seeing things, but this was Abby. He closed his eyes and thought back to when he caught a glimpse of her. She had short black hair, milky colored skin, and the most beautiful black eyes. "Maybe, but I can still see her."

"Was she pretty?"

"Prettiest girl I've ever seen. Maybe she was an angel. She had skin as white as snow."

"Well, you better put your angel away, because here comes trouble."

Eli was little more than a blur as he rounded the bend at great speed. Sam's chest tightened as if in a vice. *Oh crap!*

Eli slid to a stop in front of him. "What's wrong?" Eli said with urgency. His eyes darted from Sam to Abby and then began scrutinizing the area as if he expected an army to come down on them. "When Abby jumped out the truck window, I knew something must be wrong."

He doesn't know, thought Sam as he glanced at Abby. She didn't tell him. For a fleeting moment, he thought he might get out of this, but the thought of lying made his stomach hurt again.

Sam looked guiltily at the two full buckets by the waterfall. "I thought since I finished my chores, I would take a swim."

Eli's tense shoulders relaxed a bit when his gaze turned back to Sam. "Swim? Abby jumped out of a moving vehicle because you took a swim?"

Abby sat in silence. He wondered if she would back him up if he decided to lie.

"No, she jumped out because I was drowning. I caught my foot on a root."

A roller coaster of emotion flashed across Eli's face. It went from surprise, to shock, to relief, and then to anger in a matter of seconds. He opened his mouth, ready to fire the condemnation Sam guessed was coming, but instead only shook his finger until even that faded away. Eli's disappointed face disappeared when he turned to leave.

Sam expected yelling, punishment, chores doubled...something for what he had done, but no response at all turned out to be worse. He grabbed the two buckets and started after him. When they reached the cabin, Eli went straight for the truck. A pang of guilt shot through Sam when he noticed the driver's door still open and the truck running. He finished topping off the cistern while Eli and Abby unloaded the supplies from town. He was in no hurry to get inside, so he slowly climbed the ladder to close the lid on the cistern.

Eli was busy cooking supper when he bucked up enough courage to go inside. Taking advantage of Eli's turned back, he bolted for the bathroom. He didn't need a shower after the swim, but he took one anyway. When he finally emerged, Eli's and Abby's eyes burned through him. He hung his head as he sat at the table.

"What's with the glum face?"

The question caught Sam off guard. He still expected at least a scolding, but Eli's face seemed sincere. "I thought you'd be mad at me for swimming."

"What on earth for?" Eli smiled.

Sam frowned at Eli's strange response. "Well, I took a swim when I should've been training." He reasoned and added as an afterthought, "And I almost drowned."

"You had the last two buckets for your trip back. To be honest, I'm kind of surprised you hadn't sneaked in a swim earlier."

"So, you're not mad?"

"I wouldn't say mad. Maybe—scared." Eli shuffled a portion of spaghetti onto Abby's plate and then his own. "Whatever it was, I haven't felt that in quite a while. Anyway, you took a swim. No big deal. You shouldn't swim alone, but I don't have to tell you that now, do I?" Eli handed him the wooden bowl of spaghetti.

Sam vigorously shook his head as he took the bowl.

"Lessons are best learned from our mistakes. Granted, wise people learn from their mistakes while fools tend to keep repeating them."

"I won't be swimming alone again; that's for sure."

Eli smiled as he dished out stewed carrots to his and Abby's plates before passing the bowl to Sam. "You're already showing wisdom."

Sam smiled. His relief prompted him to dish out an extra amount of carrots, which was unusual since he didn't like them much.

"I have to keep reminding myself you're a kid. I've been training you hard, like a man, and you've taken it well, but I think it's time I let loose of the reins a bit."

Sam was in mid shovel when he furrowed his brow at Eli, spaghetti hanging out the corners of his mouth.

"From now on, we'll be taking Sundays off. You'll be free to do anything you like, after church, that is." He frowned as Sam used his fingers to shove the rest of his food into his mouth. "Probably wouldn't hurt to teach you some manners."

Sam excitedly swallowed. "I get a day off?"

"Yes, after church." Eli raised an eyebrow to emphasize that point. "Our bible studies on Sundays are great, but you need to socialize with someone besides an old warrior and a talking dog. A real church is the perfect place to start. It would do you good to get out in the world."

Sam had gone to church before. He had never missed a Sunday at the group home. Not that he had a choice, but church wasn't bad. He remembered before he had faked his recovery, he liked going since he got to be in the same room with the other kids.

"We got you some church clothes for tomorrow. Abby helped me pick them out. They're in the sacks by your bed." They had long since stopped calling the couch where he slept anything else. "Church is at ten, so you get to sleep in, but when I start to make breakfast, you need to get up."

The news just kept getting better and better. "I'll get up first sound," he said, grinning.

"Oh, and another thing." Eli reached under the table and brought out BK and a leather knife sheath with long strips of leather hanging from it. It looked a little funny when he put the massive sword inside the six-inch sheath. However, as Eli kept pushing BK down, it transformed into a knife that fit perfectly. "Take BK with you wherever you go, even when you skinny-dip in the spring." Eli smirked a little as he handed him the knife, but when Sam took it, Eli's smirk turned into a wide grin. "You wouldn't have needed that pretty girl if you had this strapped on."

Sam glared at Abby.

Abby stopped licking her plate to innocently turn to Sam. "What?"

"Do you have to tell everything you know?"

"No, only the good stuff." Her mouth dropped open into a pant, but she wasn't hot, she was smiling. "Tell Eli how pretty she was. I'm sure he'd like to hear the story firsthand."

Eli chuckled and pushed back from the table to get up. "Clean the kitchen and get to bed. We have a long—" Eli stopped himself and smiled. "We have absolutely nothing to do tomorrow."

That sounded awesome to Sam. However, he had a tiny uncomfortable twinge in his chest. *It always seems as if I get into trouble when I have nothing to do.*

11—HALLELUJAH

Sam didn't know whether it was the routine or the excitement of going somewhere new, but he woke at dawn. He tried to go back to sleep, but the cracks and pops of the cabin put him on edge. Eventually, he gave up and decided to prepare breakfast instead. He'd been helping Eli cook for three months now, so he knew what to do. Start with the coffee.

Once he got the coffee brewing, he dumped a big chunk of bacon into the cast-iron pan and turned on the stove. The trick to good bacon was to cook it slowly, allowing it to sizzle, but not pop. He greased another pan for cooking eggs. Sunny-side up was his goal, but he broke some of the yokes, so he stirred them into scrambled.

He smiled with pride as he inspected the table. Sam poured a mug of coffee to put next to Eli's plate. Eli emerged as if he'd rung a bell, rubbing his belly, and sniffed with his eyes closed.

"Mmmm, smells good." Eli opened his eyes, grinning at Sam. "I give you a day off, and instead of sleeping, you decide to cook us breakfast." He eagerly sat down and took his first sip of coffee.

Abby jumped up at Eli's voice and pounced into her chair. She was always perky, especially in the morning. Her tongue rolled around her mouth, catching the drool. "Sweet."

Sam grinned. "I couldn't sleep."

Eli took another sip of coffee. "It's a miracle."

"What?"

"I've finally found someone who can make a good cup of coffee," he said, smiling. "Now, let's see whether he can cook."

***

Sam's chest swelled from pride as he watched them eat. Breakfast may be the easiest meal to fix, but he had done a good job.

Eli poured another cup of coffee. "I think I'm going to like Sundays."

Sam started clearing the table to find Eli staring at him. "What?"

Eli pointed to Sam's leg. "There is one thing I like about you more than anything." He took a drink of coffee, closing his eyes and savoring the taste. "Even more than your ability to make good coffee." He pointed again at Sam's leg. "You listen."

Sam shrugged his shoulders and continued to clean off the table. Eli was referring to BK. He felt silly strapping the knife on for breakfast, but he was thankful he did.

***

Two hours later, they were all in Eli's truck. The blue slacks and white button-up shirt fit fine, but the tie was binding, causing Sam to tug at the collar.

"I wanted to get you a solid blue tie, but Abby wouldn't let me." He teasingly bumped her a little with his shoulder and winked at Sam.

Abby raised her hound nose up in mild annoyance. "The blue didn't match the pants."

Sam bent over to lay the yellow tie across his slacks. He had to admit the little blue diamonds matched perfectly. "It's great," he said, tugging again as he sat up.

She pawed at his hand. "Stop doing that or you'll mess up the knot."

Sam couldn't hear Eli chuckling, but his bouncing shoulders and grin gave him away.

"So, do churches let dogs go in?" asked Sam.

Abby turned from Sam to Eli. "That's OK. I'll wait outside. Surely, you can manage a church service without needing help."

"I don't know," said Eli grimly. "People are getting *saved* in church all the time." Eli grinned at Abby.

Abby turned and gave Sam a serious stare. Well, as serious as a hound can give. "If you get into trouble, just call. I'll come running."

Eli scowled, and he shook his head. He mumbled something about a joke.

Half an hour later, they drove down Main Street in Mount Jackson. Sam had his head halfway out the window, gaping at everything. The small town was no Little Rock, but more town than he'd seen in a while. He didn't want to miss a thing. "Is that the one?" he asked, pointing at a church with several cars in the parking lot.

"Nope." Eli drove on past.

A few blocks down the road, he saw another church, but before he could ask, he noticed something odd. The crowd outside the door was having a meeting, and they were all demons. He recognized the familiar darkness of them. "That's the one."

"No, I like the little white church down the road. That one is full of stuck-up hypocrites. The last time I went there, they all but told me they didn't want me back."

Sam had never been more serious in his life. "You don't have to go in, but I do."

Eli took one glance at Sam and turned into the church parking lot. "I'm guessing you have a reason?"

Sam couldn't explain why, but he knew without a doubt this was the church. It was like an overwhelming heartache that could only be satisfied by going in. He had a sneaking suspicion the demons were somehow involved. Sam nodded at Eli.

"Good enough for me." Eli grinned as he got out. "I have a feeling this will be interesting."

Abby climbed over Sam's lap, stuck her head out the window, and sniffed. "Sam, what's going on?"

"Not sure, but I have to go inside this church. It's calling me."

Sam and Eli went side by side up the steps and through the door. The small church was split into two sides of pews. The middle aisle ran straight up to the pulpit where a thin-faced man wiped the sweat off his brow. The notes he had in his hand shook. To his left stood a lovely woman and three little girls standing in line by size, but Sam's attention went to the angel to his right. This was the first time he'd seen someone have only an angel. He was the brightest angel he'd ever seen, but by his frown and crossed arms, he needed help.

Sam counted the demons. *Seven, eight, nine…*Nine in all, standing bent over whispering into…Sam had to think for a moment at what to call these men and women. "Victims" was the first thing that came to mind, but they didn't look like victims as they sat with their noses up in the air, glaring at the preacher. *And where are their angels? Given up on them, I bet.*

Sam and Eli stood silently at the back of the church.

"T-today," started the preacher nervously, "we're voting on my continuation as your pastor. I'd like to remind everyone, as the bylaws clearly state, only members are eligible to vote. So, only take one if you are a member in good standing." The preacher nodded, and a couple of boys in the front row began handing out the ballots. "The bylaws also state that time will be allowed for anyone, member or not, to make the case for my tenure. Would anyone like to speak on my behalf?" By the mere glance he gave the congregation, he didn't expect anyone to volunteer, let alone a boy in the back.

"I'd like to defend you," Sam said before he recognized his own voice. The only thing that surprised him more was his legs walking him straight up to the pulpit. Again, his mouth started talking as if he had no control. "It's high time somebody did in this den of demons." He'd never seen so many old ladies reach for their mouths. As he strolled to the pulpit, the demons hissed and glared.

In the midst of the congregation's turmoil, he took control of his mouth and whispered to the angel before turning around. "Help me if you can."

The angel grinned and started speaking. All Sam had to do was repeat his words.

"Brother Wilson has worked continuously for the last three years to bring life to this dead church. He has counseled, visited, prayed, and preached. There is not one person in here he has missed. You pay him almost nothing, but you expect everything. The virtues of this man are many, but yours are few. This man has a family to support and support he will receive. I'm not up here to talk you into keeping him. I'm here to show you your hearts."

The angel pointed out in front of Sam.

Sam pointed in the same direction as the angel. "Mrs. Jones, you pretend to give to the poor, yet somehow the money never leaves your greedy hands."

Again, Sam pointed with the angel. "Mr. Potter, cheating your brother from his rightful inheritance is so brotherly of you. Do you think he would be interested to know your mother's jewelry is in a shoebox in your closet?" A man across the aisle who looked like Mr. Potter, only a bit younger and much angrier, walked out.

Sam pointed one, two, and three in turn. "Mrs. Welch, Mrs. Selby, and Mrs. Frost. Oh, the trouble you stir with those wicked tongues. I tell you the truth, your gossiping heaps coals of burning judgment on your heads."

An elderly gentleman in back smiled at the spectacle going on, but his face changed when Sam pointed at him. "Mr. Childers, don't think I've forgotten about you. Elder of the church. Ha! You put your wife into an early grave by your selfish and harsh treatment. She wanted so little, but you denied her much. She preferred death to you. Why do you think your children never call or visit? You should be ashamed."

The old man's face turned beet red. He stood up and pointed a finger at Sam but then clutched his throat as if something were keeping him from talking. He dropped back into his pew.

"Don't worry about your audience, boy. I'll make sure they hear everything I have to say." The angel winked at Sam and then continued.

Again, Sam pointed them out one, two, and three. "Mr. Johnson, Mr. Addie, and Mr. Bryant, maybe you should explain what happened to the church building fund? Oh, that's right. You split the money between yourselves and reported the investment turned sour. Of course, when Mr. Childers caught you in the lie, he settled for a split instead. Stealing from people is one thing, but stealing from God?"

Sam had never seen so many mouths dropped open. The angel whispered one last thing in his ear. "Like I said, Brother Wilson doesn't need your vote. He's the new pastor at the little white church down the road." Sam turned toward the preacher and his family. "They have been praying for a new pastor to walk through their doors. Wouldn't it be cool if you showed up today and told them their prayers were answered?"

The angel corrected Sam's off-the-cuff interpretation, and he quickly relayed the message. "No, I mean, go *tell* the church their prayers are answered. Stand up and be brave. It's time for boldness."

Pastor Wilson's eyes shined like two pale-blue moons, staring straight at Sam. The pastor grew in height as he stood up straight and nodded firmly at the young man.

Sam started to leave the pulpit, but the angel stopped him.

"Boy, you just did what I've been trying to do over the last three years."

Sam knew he would look odd replying since he was the only one that could see the angel, but he didn't care. "What, point out their sins?"

"No, of course not. Everyone sins. I was referring to their hearts. You broke them." The angel pointed to the back of the church.

Nine angels walked through the door, literally, because the door was still closed. Each angel went to their assigned person and began whispering. The demons were throwing fits of rage, hissing and yelling at their heavenly counterparts, but the angels ignored them.

As Sam walked out of the church, he heard one girl's sweet southern drawl ring above all the others. "Hallelujah!"

He turned as the door shut, and for a brief moment, he caught a glimpse of the pastor's girls hugging their father tight.

Eli put his arm around him and squeezed. "That was exciting. How did you get the dirt on them?"

Sam continued toward the truck, grinning. "I only repeated what Mr. Wilson's angel said."

Sam and Eli climbed into the truck, but Abby was missing. Before he could get out to search for her, she jumped in and over to her spot in the middle.

"Sorry, did I miss anything?"

Eli and Sam both cracked up laughing.

12—HIDE-AND-SEEK

Two months later, Sam and Abby sat on the porch, enjoying the beautiful view. The air was not yet crisp, but fall was coming. The mesmerizing display of green, yellow, orange, and red leaves testified strongly of this. He barely heard the game playing over Eli's yelling. Eli liked his Sunday football, though he complained some about how the players wore too many pads. Sam grinned, thinking how Eli once suggested the game would be more interesting if they had weapons.

"Do you want to watch football or play?" Sam already knew how Abby would answer and dressed for the game. He was in full camouflage with BK strapped to his belt. The shirt would be hot, but the long sleeves helped protect his arms from the brush and briars.

"Let's play hide-and-seek," suggested Abby. Her casual tone didn't hide her quivering excitement.

She wasn't fooling him. She loved that game because she always won. After all, a hound tracked by scent, but today he had a few tricks up his sleeve. "OK, but you have to give me an hour head start this time."

"An hour or a day, I'll still find you."

"We'll see." Sam grinned. "If you don't find me in two hours, I win."

"OK, one, two, three, GO!" Abby wagged her tail so fast her whole backside swung.

"Hold on, before I go you have to sit with Eli. I told him he had to keep an eye on you for an hour."

"Oh, Sam, you don't trust me?" She sat down and made her eyes and mouth droop in a sad way.

Sam trusted her with the important things, like his life, but she was ruthless when she played games. She was quite devious when she wanted to be. "Of course I trust you," Sam said, scratching her behind the ears and grinning. "I trust you to cheat every chance you get. Now, get in the cabin."

She indignantly jerked her head away and opened the door with her mouth. "I don't have to cheat to find you. For that little comment, I'll find you in an hour and a half." She slammed the cabin door behind her.

Sam chuckled at her performance. He had no doubt she was already scheming how to escape from Eli, but he'd already taken care of that. He'd given Eli strict instructions to tie her to his leg and start a stopwatch. He didn't figure she would take it well, and by the growls inside the cabin, he was right. He smiled.

Eli wasn't only helping by making sure she didn't leave early, he had also taught Sam how to keep Abby from reading his thoughts. It was a matter of concentration. Earlier in the week, he had tested his newfound control by insulting her in his head, and she never responded. Abby *always* responded to his teasing. He kept his new skill hidden by letting a few well-chosen thoughts pass by throughout the week. His internal clock ticked loudly in his head. It was time to put his plan into action.

The plan was good, at least in his opinion. He had set it up for the last two Sundays. Abby had found him both times, but not before finishing what he set out to do. He put up a temporary swing across a crevasse on the mountain to the west. When he heard Abby's bawl getting close, he used this early warning to stop his work and backtrack. He didn't want Abby to reach the crevasse and discover his plan.

He had come across the crevasse by accident trying to elude Abby. The giant crack in the mountain spanned at least twenty feet across and several hundred feet down. One side was much lower than the other, and he figured if he tied a rope to one of the lower side's tree limbs, he could swing across without hitting the side of the mountain. The next week, he tied a rope high up in a tree on the lower side. He then threw the loose end across the crevasse to be ready for next week. He figured, even if Abby realized how he crossed, it would take her more than an hour to climb down and go around.

As he ran, he hoped the rope was still lying on the high side. He comforted himself by remembering his backup plan. Even if something had dislodged the rope, he could try again in two more weeks.

Sam ran through the woods with ease and speed. The months of training had made him strong and agile. He maneuvered the narrow animal trails at a quick pace. Animals knew best how to get around in the thick underbrush, and Sam planned to take every advantage. The incline started to steepen, and he dug in. He wanted to be at the crevasse before Abby's first howl. His heart pounded in his ears, more from excitement than effort.

He climbed the small crest in front of the crevasse, and his eyes searched. Relief and excitement flooded his senses when he spotted the rope. Sam quickly unbuttoned his long-sleeve shirt and took it off. He had another trick before he swung across. His T-shirt was soaked in sweat from the long run. It reeked as he pulled the shirt over his head.

He put a fist-sized rock inside the shirt and tied off the holes. Just as he finished tying the twenty-foot rope to his T-shirt, he heard Abby's cry. He paused for only a moment. Although it took him an hour to reach this spot, Abby would be here in less than thirty minutes. Using the rope, he dragged the smelly T-shirt on the ground and over the side of the cliff. Last week when he threw the rope over the crevasse, he spotted a small cave below the ledge. He thought if he dropped his shirt down by the cave, he would fool her into thinking he had climbed down to hide. He let the shirt drop, making sure it swung backward into the cave.

Next, he put his long-sleeve shirt back on. A piece of duct tape marked the spot where the rope came even with the far ledge. Grabbing too low would cause him to hit the side of the cliff. Carefully, he measured several feet above the tape and positioned his hands tightly. Heights didn't bother him, but peering over the ledge made his head swim. Abby's bawl sounded closer, and he swung. He glided to a stop exactly where he had planned on the other side. He scurried up the tree and untied the rope. He hid the rope behind a rock and took off down the other side of the mountain. Abby had a heck of a nose, and he didn't want to be close when she arrived.

Sam was well up on another mountain when Abby howled. He smiled, because Abby thought she had found him by the way she barked. Sam deceitfully allowed that thought to pass through to her. *Oh, drat. She found me.*

"Yes, I found you in less than an hour and a half. You might as well come out. How did you get down there anyway?"

I thought you said you didn't read my mind when we played this game?

"Who said I read your mind?"

You responded to what I thought. So, you cheated. Do you admit defeat?

After a long pause, she replied. "Oh, you tricky boy. I should have known this was too easy. You left marks on the tree where you used a rope to swing across. Defeat? Never. You better be running, because here I come."

Sam shut her out of his mind, and his grin turned down. *Surely, she can't catch me now.* He wondered if she were strong enough to jump the crevasse. He set his jaw as he bolted through the woods. The timber blurred from his quickened pace. *She'll have to fly if she plans to catch me.*

He didn't stop running for the next hour. When he had no doubt he had won, he stopped and rested by a spring. The water tasted sweet, and he drank too much, but he didn't care. He'd won. Being in shape was one thing, but running full-out through rough woods had a price. His muscles were already beginning to tighten.

He looked around as he tried to get comfortable with his back against a tree. The place wasn't familiar. Just a tweak of worry tingled his skin, and then he realized Abby would find him. She never got lost.

Thirty minutes later, he decided to get up and stretch his stiff muscles. However, something moved to his left. The black object made him think Abby had arrived, and he started to yell out, but then a person came into view. It was someone dressed in a black cowl. Limbs and leaves partly blocked his view. However, when the mysterious person bent over to fill a bucket from the stream, he caught a glimpse of her face inside the dark hood. It wasn't more than a glance, but he thought he recognized her. *The girl who saved me.* He leaned forward, but she turned and walked away.

He got up and stalked her. He didn't fear her, but Eli trained him to be cautious. "If you observe people when they think they are alone, you can tell a lot about them," he would always say. Sam definitely wanted to know more about this girl.

He didn't have to follow her long before he realized she was headed for a small shack in the middle of a meadow. He stayed hidden in the timber about fifty yards away. She opened the rickety door and disappeared inside.

This was the perfect opportunity to talk to the girl. Abby was nowhere to be seen, and Eli was back at the cabin. Although Abby saving him from drowning made sense, he also knew what he saw that day. Sam headed for the shack.

Looking over his shoulder for Abby, he turned back and rapped smartly on the door.

"Come in."

Sam reached for the door, but then stopped. A prickly sensation climbed his spine until the hair on the back of his neck felt as if it were standing on end. He glanced toward the timber.

The voice from the shack beckoned sweetly. "Please, come in for a visit."

Her soothing voice deadened the warning bells in his head until curiosity defeated caution. He unlatched the door and pushed inside. The creaky door almost wobbled off the hinges. He allowed his eyes to adjust to the darkness. The girl had her back to him as she poured the bucket into a basin. She appeared taller than what he had imagined. He stepped a few paces inside. "I was wondering if we had met before."

"I don't know," she said as she turned, pulling back her cowl. "Have we?"

The woman had the same round face and pixy black hair, but not the cute button nose and creamy skin of the girl who had saved him from drowning. "Oh, I'm sorry. I was mistaken." He backed up to leave, but the door had shut. Something about the woman made him anxious. He tried to open the door, but the latch wasn't working. "I don't guess you have a daughter?" He continued to work the latch and flinched when she put her warm hand on his.

"It's a little tricky. You have to pull, then lift up." She moved his hand to show him. When the latch broke free, she let go of his hand and opened the door. "No, I'm sorry to say I don't have any family. Wish I did. My name is Peony."

Sam had the urge to run out the door but instead decided to be polite. "Hi, I'm Sam."

She shook the hand he offered. Her hazel eyes squinted with her smile, but they had a hint of sadness to them. "How did you come to find my place?"

"I was playing hide-and-seek with my friend, and I got lost."

"Oh my, do you think your friend is lost?"

"No, Abby never gets lost. I was kind of waiting for her to find me." Sam awkwardly kicked at the corner of the door.

"I'm an expert for helping the lost." She took his hand into her own and started looking at his palm. "You're about five miles east of where you live." The woman giggled with surprise. "Also, your friend Abby, who is very beautiful by the way, is about a mile away and closing fast." She smiled sweetly and gestured in a direction. "If you go that way, you'll run into her in no time."

"Oh," said Sam in shock. "Thank you." He nodded and walked out the door.

Peony peered around the edge of the door. "Please come visit again if you ever need my help or would like to talk. I get so lonely."

Sam glanced back to wave, and his heart skipped a beat. *She's possessed!*

13—PEONY THE FORTUNE-TELLER

The demon's gloating smile irritated Sam, but he was careful not to show it. Her large body made an eerie frame around Peony, as if she had the poor woman trapped inside her. Sam finished waving at Peony and discovered the truth. It was the other way around. Peony began to shut the door and the demon disappeared inside *her*. He started walking to the spring and flipped the imaginary switch in his head so Abby could read his thoughts. *Abby?*

"You learned to shut me out, didn't you?"

Yes, are you close?

"I just found where you rested by a spring. You're not running again, are you? I admit you won this time. We need to head back before dark."

"No, I'm right here." Sam met Abby on the path from the spring.

Abby ran up to him and rubbed her neck on his leg. He scratched behind her ears. "Hey, you weren't barking."

"Yeah, I figured out you shut me out of your head, so I shut my mouth. I didn't want to give you warning I was coming."

Sam bent to his knees and put both hands into scratching her ears. She groaned in appreciation. "Do you know where we are?"

"Of course I do. Down the path is the fortune-teller's shack and about two hundred yards north is the road we take to town. The road will be a couple miles longer, but easier than the timber."

"So, you know Peony?"

"Who?"

"Peony is the fortune-teller."

"Oh, that's her name. Eli mentioned her once. I guess she got ran out of town, so she came up here. I've watched her a few times, and she had a bunch of customers. She must be pretty good at telling fortunes."

"I bet she is," he said darkly. "She read my palm and told me I was five miles east of the cabin and you were about a mile away." He frowned as he recalled something strange. "But she was wrong when she called you a girl."

Abby pulled back from his petting to stare at him. "Well, I am a *girl* dog."

"I guess that's it." He smiled at his friend. "She did say one other thing about you. She said you were beautiful."

Abby laughed. "She got the most important part right."

"The only problem is that she's possessed."

"Oh, how terrible, but it makes sense. She has inside information."

Sam wanted to remember how to get back. "Would it be faster cutting across the mountain?"

"Yes, if you can keep up with me." Abby bolted due east.

***

Sam and Abby burst through the cabin door to find Eli sleeping through another ballgame.

"Eli, wake up," said Sam, shaking him.

Abby put her feet up on the recliner arm and licked his face.

"Cut that out," he said, pushing her back. He looked at the clock and then to Sam. "Hey, did you win?"

"Yes, I won, but we have some important news."

Eli's grin turned into a yawn, and he stretched his arms above his head. Shaking his head, he lowered the footrest and sat up. "OK, tell me the news that is so important to interrupt my ballgame. It was just getting good."

Abby dropped her front paws to the ground. "Give me a break. You don't even know who's playing."

Eli glanced at the TV and sheepishly grinned. "Huh, must have dozed off. Well, what's the news?"

"When I was waiting for Abby to catch up, I saw this woman by a stream. I thought she was the—it doesn't matter who I thought she was. It turned out to be Peony the fortune-teller."

"Good gracious, that's quite a piece you covered. Must be at least four miles."

"Five," Sam said, grinning. "At least, that's what Peony said when she read my palm."

Eli frowned. "You let her read your palm?"

He shrugged his shoulders. "I didn't mean to. She just grabbed my hand. The important news is *how* she can tell the future."

Eli's frown deepened. "She's got a demon, doesn't she?"

"You knew?"

"Suspected," he said grimly. "She was either good at conning people, or she had help. That's too bad. I kind of liked her."

Sam frowned. "Can't we help her?"

"You can't help those who don't want it. Let me ask you a question. Any angels hanging around?"

"No, but she didn't seem evil."

"Was the demon outside talking to her or was she possessed?"

"Possessed."

Eli sat up a little straighter. "Well, that's something. If she's possessed, we might have a chance. This is important. Why did you talk to her in the first place?"

Sam didn't want to go there, but Eli left him no choice. "I thought she was the girl who saved me."

Eli glanced at Abby.

"I followed her to a shack and knocked on the door. When I found out she wasn't the girl, I left."

"Where was the demon?"

"She only popped her head out when I left."

Eli rubbed his beard in thought. "OK. We'll give it a try, but there's nothing we can do if she doesn't want our help." Eli stood up and headed to the back of the cabin. "I need to get a few things. You two get in the truck."

***

At dusk, Eli pulled onto a lane off the main road. The dark shack flickered with candlelight. Eli parked the truck and turned to Sam. "Even if she lets us, this won't work without the name of the demon. In the past, I had to force the name out by torture. I don't want to put Peony through the pain if I can help it. With your ability, maybe we can trick this one into giving it up, so don't let on you can see or hear the demon."

Sam nodded.

Eli walked through the shack door as if storming a castle.

Peony stood by her table. Instead of shock or anger for someone so rudely invading her home, she smiled. "Eli, how wonderful for you to visit. Oh my, you brought Sam and Abby. This is turning into a party. Should I make tea?"

"I'm not going to beat around the bush. You're possessed by a demon. We will exorcise it if you want. This demon, whether you know it or not, is why you can tell fortunes. If we're successful, you'll have to find a new line of work. Do you want our help?"

Peony's smiling face strained, and her lips began to twitch. Erupting from her chest popped out the fatheaded

102

demon, glaring at Eli. Sam thought how lucky Eli was to not see her ugly face.

"Tell the boy about his dog," said the demon. "That will throw them off."

Peony looked down at Abby. "So beautiful you are. Does Sam know about you?"

"Do you want our help?" Eli asked in an impatient growl.

Peony glanced back at Eli, tears streaming down her agonized face. "YES, help me, please." Her body shuddered.

The demon turned and put her furious face in front of Peony. "You stupid woman! Fortune-telling is all you can do. You'll starve without me." Peony put her hand in front of her face as though she was trying to protect herself.

Sam tugged on Eli's shirt. "Maybe we can help her find a new job?"

Eli caught his meaning. "Yes, I promise we'll find you a new job."

The demon turned to Eli. "Lies! He speaks lies! I'm the only one who speaks truth. I'm your only friend."

Eli grabbed Peony's quivering shoulders. "All you have to do is give us the name."

The fat-faced demon spun her head around as if it were on a swivel. "I forbid you to speak my name."

"I—can't—tell—you," said Peony through sobs.

The demon's laughter sent chills down Sam's spine, but her mirthful expression faded as if she had thought of something awful. "And you must not show them my mark!"

If Sam hadn't heard what the demon had said, he wouldn't have noticed Peony rubbing the back of her neck.

Sam stepped up and grabbed Peony's hand. "You know, Eli, sometimes really dumb demons put their names on the neck. Let's check."

The demon screamed in rage and disappeared inside her host. Eli grabbed Peony's other arm and forced her to turn around. Her body jerked out of his hands and flew to the ceiling like gravity had somehow reversed for her. The ceiling was low, so Eli easily grabbed her around the waist, but had to use his considerable strength and weight to pull her to the floor. He lay on the floor, trying to hold her still. Her arms thrashed, and her legs frantically kicked.

"Sam, get the name quick. I can't hold her much longer." Peony started punching Eli in the face so hard his head pounded the floor like a sledgehammer. Instead of anger, he smiled up at her with blood-stained teeth. "Hang on, Peony. We're almost there."

Sam pulled back the cowl of her cloak and Peony hissed and snapped at him with her teeth. Eli grabbed her hair to hold her head still. Unfortunately, Peony sunk her teeth into Eli's ear. "Abby," he said hoarsely, "I need you to change and hold her legs."

"But, Eli—" started Abby, but he cut her off.

"He should know, anyway, and hurry. She's a handful."

"Oh, all right." Abby bound past them and went behind a three-fold privacy screen. A moment later, a girl's hand reached over the top and grabbed a cloak off the screen.

Eli yelled with strain. "Anytime you're ready. Come on."

"This isn't how I planned to tell you," Abby said, and not in Sam's head for the first time. The black-headed girl who had saved him from drowning emerged. "I can transform into a human."

Sam's mouth dropped in shock. "I told you I saw a girl."

"If you two don't mind, I'm about to lose an ear!"

Abby rushed to hold Peony's legs. Sam was still in shock at seeing Abby this way and had to shake his head to focus. He pulled back the cloak again as Peony jerked one way and another, but this time he could see the mark. "It looks like a tattoo of a pig on its back drinking from a bottle." Sam drew closer to read the letters on the tattooed bottle. "The pig's drinking rum."

Peony screamed with rage.

Still holding her short-cropped hair, Eli pulled her head from his face. She took most of his ear in the process, spitting a chunk to the floor. "In my bag, get the ropes."

Sam retrieved them while Eli grabbed her wrists and spun her over so her arms were now behind her. He quickly bound them together. The rope touching her skin started to sizzle and smoke. He took another rope from Sam and bound her feet. Peony, or rather the demon inside her, seemed to be getting weaker.

"Handy rope this is," Eli said, picking her up and laying her across the table. "Soaked in holy water. It drains their strength for a short time." Eli smiled and gave Sam a wink. "I think I know the demon's name." He raised his eyebrows as if he asked a question. "Pigrum?"

The demon squealed when he said it and Sam grinned back. "I think you're right."

Eli chuckled at Sam's conformation. "Pigrum means 'lazy' in Latin."

Sam noticed Eli's ear was back in place, and he didn't seem to be bleeding.

"OK, almost done. Give me BK."

Sam slipped BK out of his sheath and handed him the knife. BK started to glow.

Peony's body was now limp and turned a little sideways because of her hands tied behind her back.

"Get the jar in the bag. Unscrew the lid, but don't let the spider escape. When I tell you, remove the lid and stick the mouth of the jar over her right eye, sealing it against her skin."

Sam retrieved the jar and got ready.

Eli grimly took BK and made two deep slashes in his left palm, pooling the blood into a red, liquid cross. He set BK on the table. "My blood is like poison to a demon. The demon enters and leaves a body through the eyes. Eyes are the windows to the soul. To make sure the demon comes out her right eye, I'm going to put some of my blood around her left. Get ready." Eli dipped a finger into his blood and made a red circle around her left eye. Her body shook violently when he placed his bloody palm on her forehead.

"PER SANGUINEM CHRISTI, PIGRUM POTEST ABIIT!" Eli glanced at Sam. "Now!"

Peony's mouth grew wide, and her eyes bulged. Sam removed the lid and pressed the opening tight around her right eye. A rush of wind filled the shack and then silence.

Eli caught her head before it hit the floor. "It's done."

Sam frantically started to put the lid on the jar so the demon wouldn't escape.

Eli smiled. "No hurry, Pigrum can't get out unless you break the jar. Take your time."

Sam slowed down and managed to screw the lid on tight. The spider was on its back, legs twitching. He was sure the spider was brown before and figured the demon had turned it black. "I guess the demon is in the spider now?"

"Yes," Eli replied as he untied the ropes from the unconscious woman.

"How can we be sure?"

The spider flipped over and began to crawl around.

Eli gently lifted Peony from the floor. "Does she still have the demon's mark?"

Sam examined the back of her neck. Only moments ago, he had clearly seen what looked like a dark tattoo. "No, it's gone."

"And so is Pigrum. Well, gone from her anyway." Eli then carried Peony to the bed in the corner of the shack. "I'll come back to stay with her once I drop you two off at the cabin. I'll bring her for breakfast if you can have one ready?" Eli grinned at Sam.

Sam smiled in relief as he put the ropes and the jar into Eli's bag. "I'll make the coffee, but I think Abby should cook, now that she has hands." He turned to the girl, but found only the dog.

"Sorry. I only turn into a human when needed. You'll have to fix breakfast on your own."

Sam frowned. "Well, at least I'm not crazy."

Eli raised an eyebrow. "Remember, Pigrum can only escape if you break the jar."

"I will." Sam headed for the door. "Are exorcisms always this rough?"

Eli chuckled. "That was the easiest exorcism I ever did, thanks to you."

14—ADVANCED SWORD TRAINING

On the third day of trying, Eli found Peony a job as a
secretary in the Mount Jackson elementary school. Her
past reputation preceded her, so it took a little persuasion
and the help of Pastor Wilson to get the job. Turns out,
Mr. Wilson was on the school board and was more than
willing to help. Although Sam knew better, Mr. Wilson felt
indebted to Sam for his new job at the little white church.

Sam wasn't so lucky. He had never mentioned it, but he
was excited to go to a real school for the first time.
Unfortunately, Eli had other plans. Instead of going to
school, school came to him. Eli made his thoughts clear
about the subject. "No use wasting the whole day when
there is only enough material for half." Eli meant what he
said, because after he homeschooled Sam in the morning,
he continued training him in the afternoon.

Sam was now in the middle of advanced sword
training, which was a fancy way of saying he had some
hard, tedious work to do. The training consisted of
removing stumps in the front yard with BK. The logic was
clear. Hack a million times and you'll get stronger at
swinging a sword. He'd already encountered this type of
training before, and it wasn't fun. At his third day in, he

was only half done with his first stump. For the longest while, picturing Tanas as the stump helped him to slash away, but even that wore thin after a while. He paused to count the rest of the stumps for the hundredth time, hoping each time there would be less.

Only have thirty-seven more after this one, he thought dryly.

Usually, Abby kept him company, but she wasn't around today. Since the night they exorcised Pigrum from Peony, Abby hadn't once turned back into her human form. She explained she had only transformed into a human twice. The other time being when she had saved him from drowning. He had suggested that maybe she only needed practice to be able to change at will, but she didn't seem to try very hard. Apparently, she could only turn human when there was a need greater than doing the dishes or for the curiosity of a boy.

He sighed and drew BK back to strike that ever-wicked stump, but instead, chills ran down his spine. A barrage of yelping culminated into a mournful, high-pitched howl that echoed from the west.

Abby? he asked in his head but only got another howl in reply. *Are you OK?* He didn't know whether the howl came from Abby or not, but he couldn't take the chance. In one swift move, he sheathed BK and took off like a shot in the direction of the howls.

The crying sound of pain carried well through the mountain, disguising the distance. Sam flew through the timber at speeds he didn't realize he could go. His mind locked in fear that Abby was in trouble, and he had to get there fast. He had to save her.

Just as he crested the ridge before the crevasse, he tripped on a root. His momentum carried him through the air, and his heart caught in his throat. Screaming in silent terror, he flew straight toward a full-grown wolf crouched near to the ground. His voice didn't work, but his arms and legs moved in overtime. His frantic back peddling didn't help much until he hit the ground. He skidded to a stop, inches from the snarling wolf.

He didn't know why the wolf hadn't attacked, but he wouldn't sit around and wonder. Slowly, he backed away, jerking when the wolf snapped its vicious snout. Curiously, it didn't advance. When he stood up, he figured out why. The wolf wore a rust-colored noose—a snare.

The wolf must have decided Sam wasn't a threat because it began clawing at the steel cable looped around its neck. Eli had shown him how to set snares for survival, but mainly for smaller animals like rabbits and squirrels. He knew the wolf would choke itself to death if he didn't do something quick. The wolf mournfully howled and lay on its side. Its labored breathing became shallow.

He thought he might try to release the snare. Carefully, he approached the wolf. It didn't move, so Sam reached for the cable. Although its eyes were open, they were hazy, and its tongue lolled about. This encouraged Sam to continue. Gently, he grabbed the cable with his left hand and worked the catch to widen the loop. When he had enough slack, he worked the cable off the wolf's neck. Just as he cleared its long snout, the wolf snapped viciously, but his chazah kicked in with a warning. He jerked his hand back, and for a second, he thought the wolf missed, but he was wrong. The wolf's razor sharp teeth had sliced through the top of his hand and when he yanked his hand away the skin peeled to his knuckles. He hadn't felt a thing until he pushed the skin back into place.

The wolf jumped up. Sam awkwardly retreated while holding his bleeding hand. He fell into the leaves as the wolf took advantage and loomed menacingly over him.

Great, I save your life and now you're going to kill me. Sam held his hands out in front of him to guard his neck and face. He wanted to reach for BK, but he was certain the wolf would attack if he lowered his guard.

Something growled behind him. His first thought was Abby. At this point, he didn't much care what growled, because the wolf ducked its head, whimpered, and fled. Sam thought it strange since the wolf was at least twice the size of Abby, but then again, she could be ferocious.

Clutching his bleeding hand, he sat up. "I'm sure glad you came when you did. I was almost a goner. This is my reward for saving its mangy life." Sam turned to show her his hand, but Abby wasn't standing on the ridge. Deep rumblings radiated through his bones. Sam's eyes felt as if they were about to bulge right out of their sockets as he stared down the giant mountain lion on the ridge.

He jumped up and drew BK out of its sheath. His hand hurt, but the huge amount of fear coursing through his veins deadened the pain. When BK grew into a sword, he supported his weak hand by gripping it with both.

The golden cat was huge, at least twice the size of the wolf. He followed its pacing along the ridge with BK. *Abby, time to save me again.* "Nice kitty. You don't want to eat me. I'm all skin and bones." Too late, Sam realized he wasn't the only one drawn in by the painful cries of the wolf. Now that he had turned the wolf loose, he was next on the menu. "Hey, your meal went that way." Sam pointed BK in the direction the wolf had taken, but the lion had eyes only for him. "Yeah, the boy can't run as fast as a wolf."

The cat's pacing grew shorter as though building up to something, and he had a good idea what would happen when it stopped. He glanced at the crevasse and, for a fleeting moment, considered jumping. The crevasse spanned at least twenty feet, but the other side was much lower. *My momentum might carry me.*

Sam's chazah warned him the mountain lion was going to attack. Sam wielded BK out in front of him. He flicked his sword back and forth a couple more times in warning. The cat's yellow ears flattened, and it let loose a bloodcurdling scream that vibrated the ground, but thankfully it began pacing again. Sam watched and realized the huge cat edged forward with each turn.

The top of the ridge was a little more than ten yards and the cat had almost cut that distance in half. *Wish I had that rope.*

He had to make a decision. Run and jump or stay and fight. He stepped forward and swung BK once again. The cat's reflexes were unbelievable, easily avoiding his blade. He didn't have a choice. If he tried to fight, he would lose.

Sam noticed the cat retreated a few feet each time he swung. If he just turned and ran for the cliff, the cat would be on him before he could jump. Sam took a deep breath and brought the sword up to his left. He stepped forward and waved it from left to right. He then stepped again, swinging right to left, fully extending his arms and letting the momentum turn him around. Without hesitation, he sprinted for the cliff and leaped at a full run. The cat's claws raked across his back as his legs churned in the air. The relief Sam felt from avoiding the jaws of the cat quickly turned to horror. He wasn't going to make it. He hit the side just below the ledge. In desperation, he thrust BK into a thin crack in the rock wall.

The sword sank tightly to the hilt, but bouncing off the wall shook his grip loose. As his body rebounded, his foot found enough traction to push him upward. He barely managed to regain his hold on BK's handle. Painfully, he brought up his injured hand to strengthen his grip. The ledge was at least four feet above him. He had rock climbed with Eli enough to recognize this wall was too smooth. *At least I got away from the cat.* The sky went dark. Over his head sailed the mountain lion. *Maybe it's a good thing I didn't make it.*

If he could hang on long enough, he knew Abby or even Eli would eventually find him, but his grip was already beginning to fail. *Abby! Where the heck are you? I'm dying here!* The rock face bulged some at his feet. His toes barely fit, but it was enough to take some of the weight off his injured wrist.

The cat's huge head peered over the ledge. It reached for him with one of its paws, its claws almost reaching his hands, like a kitten reaching for a toy. He knew he couldn't hang on forever, so he took a chance. Still holding BK in one hand, he grabbed its leg with the other and pulled. He wanted to pull the cat off the ledge and let it fall to its death. However, the mountain lion didn't budge. Instead, it started backing up.

Sam went over his options. He couldn't survive the fall, and his chances of beating such a deadly predator were not much better, but at least he *had* a chance. The cat continued to lift him upward, but his grip began to slip. He would have to either release its leg or BK, and then he had an idea.

"Knife," he commanded. BK shrunk to knife size. He pulled it loose from the wall and sank the razor-sharp blade through the bone of the cat's leg above his other hand. The lion screamed in pain, jerking Sam onto the ledge. "Sword," he yelled.

BK grew into a sword, shattering the cat's leg. It reeled backward, and for the first time, fear showed in those yellow eyes. He jumped to his feet. Grabbing BK with both hands, he pulled the sword to his left, ripping it free. He continued the motion in a circle over his head while the cat was still in shock. He stepped forward and brought BK down across its neck. Its heavy body thumped to the ground.

Afraid it might somehow revive, he stood ready, staring at its body until its tail stopped flailing.

"I see your advanced sword practice is going well," said Eli coarsely.

Sam looked up at Eli and Abby standing on the ledge across the crevasse. Abby was panting heavily and Eli rested with his hands on his knees, sucking wind. He glanced at the cat again before addressing Eli. "I don't suppose you remembered the chocolate cupcakes?" Sam tried to mirror Eli's casual tone, but his shaky voice gave him away.

Abby paced at the ledge. "I knew I shouldn't have gone to town. Did the lion injure your hand?"

Sam glanced at the hanging flap of skin. Now that the danger was passed, his hand hurt, and for the first time, he noticed the stinging warm sensation on his back. "No, the wolf did that, but the cat might have scratched me." He turned to show them.

Eli paused before answering. "Yeah, it might have gotten you a bit." Eli's tone seemed a little too calm. "We better get that looked at. How did you get across, anyway?"

Sam grew weak. He tried to put BK into his sheath, but he missed the opening, dropping the sword to the ground. He stared in confusion as the sword rose up in the air, turned into a knife, and then put itself into his sheath. *How cool*, he thought, smiling weakly. "I jumped."

Eli said something to Abby he couldn't make out but then replied louder, "You don't say. That's quite a jump."

"I fell short, but BK saved me." The ground trembled under his feet, so he dropped to his knees before he fell.

Abby yelled out. "Are you OK?"

He could hear the concern in Abby's voice, but he didn't have the strength to reply. His vision narrowed as if he were looking through a shrinking pipe until everything went black.

15—ELI'S VISION

The faces staring down at him seemed strange as he blinked several times to clear his vision. In her usual spot, Abby warmed his side. He closed his eyes again and recognized the small ache in his back where the cushions met on the couch. He was home. His muscles relaxed, and he opened his eyes.

The faces were not as strange as he had thought. Dr. Prawn sat on a kitchen chair up close to the couch. Eli stood behind her. Another man hovered over the back of the couch. He had never seen him before, and though ginormous, his face was kind.

"Can you tell me who I am?" asked Dr. Prawn in her usual curt tone. Her top lip curled as if enduring a terrible odor.

Stretching a bit, Sam noticed his muscles were sore, but the good kind of sore you get after training.

Her patience grew short. "Samuel, do you recognize me?"

Dr. Prawn was a healer, so he reasoned his injuries must have been bad, but he felt fine now. Although she was a cranky pile of bones who hated dogs, a pang of rejection stirred when he remembered the last time he saw her. He thought she would be his new mother one second, and the next, she was running into the airport. Hanging on to Abby, he swung his legs over the side and put them on the floor. "Oh, Abby, Ma has come home to us."

Dr. Prawn's eyes widened for an instant and then narrowed with suspicion. Before she had a chance to reply, he lunged, wrapping his arms around her spindly frame in a tight hug. "I missed you, Ma." He did it as a joke, figuring she would hate it, but surprisingly, and for the shortest of moments, she hugged back. She quickly recovered from her lapse and pried him off, shoving him back to the couch.

"Oscar, we're leaving." She briskly stood up, brushing at the wrinkles in her pantsuit. "He's obviously recovered and no longer needs our services."

"Yes, ma'am." The big man nodded, grinning and showing a big gap between his front two teeth.

Eli pleaded as he followed her to the door. "Oh, Penny, don't go. We haven't had breakfast yet."

Sam couldn't help himself. "Ma, don't leave us again. I promise I'll be good."

Eli scowled in his direction, but Sam caught a glimpse of humor in his eyes.

Abby nudged him with her nose. "I like her even less than you, but she did save your life."

Regret wrenched in his stomach. He stood up. "Dr. Prawn, I'm sorry. I won't joke anymore."

She paused at the door and turned.

"Please, let me fix you breakfast. It's the least I can do."

"Smelling that foul dog all night has made me lose my appetite." She turned to leave.

"Thank you" was all he could think to say, but it was enough.

Dr. Prawn paused, nodding. Her mouth was almost in a straight line, which was quite an improvement from her usual frown. "You're welcome."

Eli and Abby followed her out the door as Oscar held it open. As Sam followed, Oscar caught him by sticking out his hand. When his catcher's-mitt-sized hand touched his chest, Sam got a warm tingling sensation.

"Don't ya go worryin' about her leavin'. She's got a good heart. She just don't like showin' it. Ya got a good'n too. I can feel it. Besides, she's been needin' a hug for the longest time and danged if ya didn't give her a dandy."

He knew the man was big, but he hadn't realized how big. Oscar's head reached about a foot above the door. Sam didn't know what to say, so he looked out the door. Eli stood watching Dr. Prawn pick her way through the rocks and clumps of grass toward a black limousine.

Oscar bent over to bring his face close to his. "Does ya know why Dr. Prawn stayed all night?"

Sam's blank stare encouraged Oscar to continue. "She couldn't heal ya all the way. She was worried 'bout ya."

Sam checked his hand and then reached for his back.

Oscar chuckled and shook his head. "Nah, she fixed yer body. She just couldn't fix yer soul. Vexed her somethin' awful, that did. O' course, the doc knew somethin' weren't right, but in the end, she couldn't fix it. Ya see, I have a gift or two m'self."

"What's wrong with my soul?" Sam reached for his chest and felt it tighten.

Oscar grabbed Sam's shoulders firmly, bringing his big smiling face up close. The warmth of his touch radiated throughout Sam's body like rushing hot water. Sam relaxed and felt exceptionally cheerful.

"Are you fixing me?"

"Nah, it's best ya do it yerself. I'm just giv'n ya a taste what it's like. I'll give ya a piece of advice that might help ya 'long the way. Hate what the evil people do, but not the people. Even that Tanas feller had a good heart once. It's yer choice if ya turn out just like him. When ya get in a tight spot and not sure what to do, trust yer heart. It'll tell ya. the important thing is ta listen." Oscar removed his hands and patted Sam on the head.

Sam had tried not to think about it, but he couldn't deny his hate for Tanas had grown steadily. It was a sticky bit of emotions that felt good and bad at the same time. He knew Eli was dead set against hate, but it was so easy to use it as fuel for training. He had even convinced himself it was OK since it was only his imagination. He wasn't really getting revenge. He was only thinking about it. Now that Oscar had pointed it out, he had known for a while that was a lie. He felt ashamed, but the guilt melted away at Oscar's jolly, gap-toothed smile.

"Don't 'spect ta whip it overnight, just work on it best ya can." Oscar winked and gave him another pat on the head.

Sam nodded, determined not to let hate get the best of him as he went out the door to stand by Eli and Abby. Oscar's enormous strides allowed him to easily overtake Dr. Prawn. She never paused as she disappeared behind the limo door he opened for her.

Eli chuckled and shook his head when Oscar drove the limo away.

"I'm guessing I was hurt worse than I thought."

"That kitty cat filleted you pretty good. By the time I got Penny here, you'd lost a lot of blood. She was worried about you." Eli paused as he gave Sam a once-over. "But you seem fine now."

Sam didn't want to get into what Oscar had said and changed the subject. "Hey, how did you get me across the crevasse?"

Eli sat in a rocker and started petting Abby. "I have another gift you haven't seen, but what's exciting is that you have the same gift."

Sam raised one eyebrow as he'd seen Eli do a thousand times.

Eli grinned. "Telekinesis."

Sam's brow creased. "You called someone?" Sam sat in one of the chairs by the table. "I didn't know we had a phone?"

Eli's grin faded. "I didn't say telephone. Any fool can use a telephone. I said *telekinesis*."

Sam wrinkled his nose. "Huh?"

"I can move things with my mind."

"What?"

Eli stopped rocking and leaned forward. "Are you sure you're all right?"

Sam shrugged his shoulders.

"What do you remember right before you passed out?"

Sam thought back. "I asked you about cupcakes—" He stopped to give Eli another raised eyebrow.

"Yes, I bought your cupcakes. Now tell me what happened."

"I put BK in my sheath, told you I jumped, dropped to my knees...That's all I remember."

Eli tilted his head. "You remember putting BK in the sheath?"

He frowned for a moment in concentration and then smiled when he remembered. "No, BK picked itself up when I dropped it. That's so cool."

"BK didn't pick *itself* up."

"I guess I was pretty bad off, so I might have been seeing things."

"No, you saw correctly. You picked BK up with your mind, not your hand. Telekinesis." Eli started rocking again, as if satisfied he got his point across.

Sam was baffled, and it must have shown on his face by the way Eli scowled.

"Just show him," Abby said, walking over and sitting down next to Sam.

Eli stopped rocking again, dug a coin out of his pocket, and laid it in the palm of his hand. "Be amazed," he said, grinning. The coin rose up, floated over to Sam, and gently rested on the table.

"That's like magic." Sam grabbed the coin. "You mean, I can do that?"

"There's no doubt you can. You just need to practice. As easily as I moved the coin, I lifted you up and over the crevasse. I floated you all the way home. It's a dang handy gift to have, and I'm glad you got it. Put the coin on the table and try moving it with your mind."

Sam dropped the coin on the table and started concentrating. He scrunched his face with strain. "What am I supposed to be thinking?"

Eli leaned forward. "First of all, quit holding your breath and relax. Now, picture in your mind what you want the coin to do."

He took a deep breath, picturing the coin moving to the far side of the table, but nothing happened.

"Your mind is like any other muscle. You only need to practice, but right now you have breakfast to cook, and after staying up all night, coffee would sure hit the spot."

Sam got up and started to hand the coin back, but Eli waved him off.

"Practice every chance you get, but don't lose it. It's a keepsake."

Sam examined the gold coin, but most of the writing was worn off.

"I won that on a bet with Robert Maynard. It's a gold doubloon."

"What was the bet?"

"I bet ol' Bob I would be the one that killed Blackbeard the pirate, and I did."

"No way!"

"I did. Blackbeard had Bob in a tight spot, but I showed up before he could finish the job." Eli rocked back in his chair in a satisfied way.

"You have to tell me the whole story." Sam started to sit back down, but Eli grabbed him by the arm, pulling him toward the door.

"Breakfast, schoolwork, and then training. After dinner, if you are still up for the story, I'll tell you the whole tale, but…"

"Yeah, yeah, I know. Daylight is for training, and nighttime is for talking." Sam grinned as he put the coin in his pocket and headed for the kitchen.

***

There weren't many chances for practicing his telekinesis until after dinner that night. He had tried moving a saltshaker during breakfast, a pencil during his school lessons, and wood chips as he chopped on the stumps in the afternoon, but nothing moved. After Eli told the pirate tale, Sam was beat. He lay on his bed, Abby at his side, with Eli's coin on his chest. He figured he'd practice his telekinesis until he fell asleep.

Thirty minutes later, his eyes were getting heavy. He let them close and tried one more time. He was too tired to imagine the coin floating off his chest to the kitchen table, so he just pictured it on the table. He had to force his eyes open to check. The coin was gone from his chest. He looked around, patting himself for the coin. When he didn't find it, he sat bolt upright, knocking Abby to the floor.

"Hey, I'm sleeping here," she complained, trying to get back up to her warm spot.

His head jerked over the back of the couch and there on the table sat the doubloon reflecting in the moonlight. "I did it. I moved the coin."

"Wonderful. Now can we go back to sleep?"

"No, you need to be my witness."

"OK, but hurry. I need my beauty sleep."

Sam wondered if closing his eyes had helped, so he closed them before trying. He pictured the coin in his hand. He smiled when he felt the coin land. "I'm not supposed to think of it moving, just where I want it. I did it again."

"You did. I saw the whole thing, so I'm your witness. Now, can we go back to sleep?"

Sam's excitement bubbled out every pore of his skin. "You can, but I think I'm going to stay up and practice a little longer." He got up, flipped the light on above the sink, and sat down at the table.

"Fine by me." Abby jumped back up on the couch, circled a couple of times, and curled up in her usual ball.

He practiced moving the coin about the cabin with his eyes shut but opened them to check. After ten successful tries, he started peeking. The coin moved anywhere he wanted, even with his eyes wide open.

From the kitchen windowsill, he willed the saltshaker to his hand, but before he caught it, he decided to tip the shaker as if he were salting his food. It turned over in air and shook a couple of times, dropping salt on the table. A laugh escaped his mouth before he could stifle it. He cringed when Eli's light came on. *Dang it, I woke him.*

Only, Eli didn't come out. He willed the saltshaker back to the windowsill, still staring down the hall, but being quiet as possible. The light escaping under Eli's door grew brighter. He began to wonder if his eyes were playing tricks on him. Blinking and rubbing his eyes, he checked again. The light grew in strength to the point he had to cover his eyes, and then a loud thump shook the cabin floor. The bright light disappeared.

Sam stood frozen for a moment, letting his eyes adjust back to the dim lighting.

Abby bound around the couch to check on Sam. "What's wrong?"

"Not sure, but there was a bright light in his room." He ran for Eli's door and yelled. "Eli, are you OK?" The door opened. He didn't know whether his eyes were still adjusting, but Eli looked ghost white standing in the doorway. "Eli?"

"I had a vision," Eli said grimly. "We've got a job to do, so both of you better get some rest." Eli shut his door.

16—CAPITOL

When Sam woke early the next morning, Abby was gone, so he decided to start breakfast. As usual, Eli emerged when the coffee was ready. Sam did a double take when Eli strolled in clean-shaven and in a suit.

"We're going to the US Capitol today, so we need to dress up." He poured his coffee and inspected the table. "The table's not set right."

Sam hadn't gathered the salt and pepper shakers from the windowsill on purpose. He'd planned on showing Eli his new skill during breakfast. He started to explain why he'd left them, but Eli continued.

"You need silverware for Abby." Eli grinned.

Out from Eli's office walked Abby in human form. She had on a simple black dress with a thin white ribbon around her waist and a white hair band. The alternating black and white material matched the differences between her dark eyes and hair with her milky white skin. Her full lips turned up into a shy smile as she took her seat at the table.

"Sam," said Eli, sitting down.

Sam turned his head toward him, but his eyes never left Abby. "Yeah?"

"If you can get a knife and a fork for Abby, we can eat this delicious breakfast before it gets cold."

"Huh?" He glanced at Eli. "Oh, yeah, OK," he said, sitting down.

Eli chuckled. "Abby needs silverware."

"Oh, right." Sam jumped up, hitting his knee on the table leg and almost caused several things to spill. "Sorry," he muttered and dashed for the silverware drawer.

"Get the salt and pepper while you're up." Eli chuckled more loudly.

Sam remembered now about showing Eli his new skill. "I left them there on purpose," he said, placing Abby's knife and fork on a napkin.

Eli's brow wrinkled as he dished out scrambled eggs.

Sitting down, Sam pictured the salt and pepper shakers on the table. They popped up from the windowsill and landed gently next to Eli's plate.

"Like I said, dang handy." Eli peppered his eggs with a grin. "That makes me feel better about this task. I didn't think you were ready, but it's not up to me."

Sam dipped out his own eggs and started to fill Abby's plate, but when he caught her smirk, he shrugged his shoulders in apology and handed over the spoon. "So, what are we supposed to do?"

Eli rubbed his chin in thought. "You need to understand how the visions work. I never get the full picture. I get scenes that I need to make happen. As long as I complete the scenes, anything else I need to do is up to me to figure out."

"Wouldn't it be easier to know exactly what we're supposed to do?" Sam chewed his bacon with less interest than usual.

Eli's brow creased. "I think it has to do with faith. If we have the faith to do what God wants without knowing why, He has the faith in us to get the job done."

Sam's stomach churned, and he stopped eating. "What were we doing in your vision?"

"I had three scenes. I'm to take you to the west front of the US Capitol building. Penny will meet us there and give us passes for watching the Senate in session. In the second scene, I drop both of you in a specific spot overlooking the Senate chamber. The third, I leave both of you there. I'll be waiting on the Capitol steps. I'm putting you in position for something, but I have no idea why. Tanas is a senator, so if I were to guess, he's somehow involved, but maybe not. You'll have to figure out what to do on your own."

Sam had a feeling of dread in the pit of his stomach. "What if I'm not smart enough?"

Eli gave an encouraging nod. "Don't you worry. You'll figure it out."

"You've done loads of these tasks, so why don't you stay and help us?" Sam's thread of hope snapped as Eli sadly shook his head.

"It makes sense that I would help you, but that's not how my visions work. Like you, I thought I had a better plan once. I did it my way instead, and three innocent lives were lost." Eli paused, and his eyes welled. Turning his gaze to his plate, he cleared his throat and took a bite of bacon.

Sam felt as if he were intruding on something personal, so he focused on his own plate. Thinking on the fly made him anxious, but that's not the reason his bowels gurgled. If Tanas was involved, this thing could get ugly quick. He patted BK for comfort.

"BK won't pass through the metal detectors, so you'll need to leave our friend in the truck." Eli pointed at his weapon.

Sam frowned. The thought of leaving BK behind was a terrible blow.

"Don't worry about your safety, that's what Abby's for."

125

Sam tried to return her smile but didn't quite manage it. He had no doubt Abby could help him if she were a dog, but a pretty girl in a dress wasn't how he'd pictured a bodyguard.

"I'll keep you safe." Abby pulled her shoulders back in a confident way.

He nodded, hoping he hid his doubt from her.

"We'll clean up the kitchen. Go put on your Sunday clothes. We need to get going." Eli's plate was barely touched when he took it to the sink.

Dread and excitement battled inside Sam as he headed for the bathroom to change.

***

The two-hour trip to the Capitol was awkward to say the least. Although Abby sat in her usual spot, her human form made Sam uncomfortable. She sat straight with her legs crossed like the girls at church. On any other road trip, she would be licking, nudging, or joking with him, but this trip, she sat staring out the windshield. He tugged on his collar to let the heat out of his shirt. He half smiled, thinking of what she would do if he scratched her behind the ears. He scrunched his face when she smirked. His stomach dropped as he wondered if she were reading his thoughts. He double-checked his imaginary switch that shut her out of his head. He was pretty sure she couldn't hear his thoughts, but why was she smirking? She turned her head. For the first time, he noticed the human Abby had the same gold flecks in her black eyes.

Sam's chazah kicked in. He saw Abby balling up her left fist and punching him in the shoulder. He instinctively caught her fist in his right hand before it happened. The sheer force of her punch knocked his hand back into his shoulder as if he hadn't blocked it at all.

"I'm still Abby, so quit looking at me like I'm an alien."

He rubbed the charley horse with his stinging hand and grinned awkwardly. "Sorry, it's just so weird."

"You don't have to tell *me* it's weird. I have to wear this silly dress and sit so funny when I usually stretch out next to you." She smirked a little, and her cheeks flushed.

"Yeah, I guess scratching your neck is out of the question?"

It was the first time she'd laughed as a girl. She brought her hand up to her mouth as if surprised. "Let's get this over with so I can turn back."

"Yeah," he agreed in a weak tone. It was weird, but strangely cool.

***

They managed to find parking and made the long walk to the Capitol building where they found Dr. Prawn waiting. She was easy to spot with Oscar standing beside her. Her nose wrinkled and nostrils flared at Abby when she handed off the passes. He wondered if Dr. Prawn still smelled dog. Sam leaned to take a sniff, but Oscar got his attention.

"Remember what I told ya," Oscar said, swatting him on the back. Sam almost lost his feet from the blow. "Trust yer heart." Oscar laughed and took off after Dr. Prawn.

Eli escorted them through the metal detectors and then to the second floor of the Senate chamber. He pointed for Abby to stand against the wall and then straightened Sam's tie. "You must sit there."

Sam nodded and took the seat Eli had shown him. "That completes the second scene. We're two-thirds done. The third scene shows me meeting you where Penny gave us the passes. I don't know how I'm supposed to make sure you show up, but that's where I'll be all the same." Eli tried to smile through his worried face. "Keep your eyes and ears sharp. Be ready for anything." Eli's face strained as if lifting something heavy. "I'd say good luck, but I don't believe in luck." He left through one of the doors by Abby.

Sam motioned her to come over.

127

She shook her head. "Eli told me to stand here."

"He didn't say you had to stay there. It's up to us now, and I want you up here."

She looked around uneasily before yielding. "What if someone tries to sneak up on you?"

"Can't sneak up on *me*." He tapped his temple and grinned before leaning over the rail. "Holy guacamole, the place is full of them."

Abby leaned over the rail next to him. "Yes, there are one hundred senators, two from each state."

"I'm not talking about *them*," he replied grimly. "I'm talking about the *demons*."

Abby looked closer, frowning. "No angels?"

"No, plenty of them too." He started scanning the chamber, counting with his finger. "About half have an angel and a demon. The old guy with the cane has only an angel, but the group over there has only demons." He pointed them out and waited until Abby nodded. "Help me keep track of them."

"Gotcha." Abby stared unblinkingly at the group he'd pointed out.

A man on the podium loudly pounded a mallet, and the senators took their seats. Sam shuddered. He doubled his efforts to find what caused it when Tanas came into view. The three demons surrounding the senator made Sam's skin crawl. They were unlike any other demons he had seen before. Demons usually appeared as humans, but these grotesque creatures were straight out of horror movies.

The biggest one stood at least ten feet tall and was covered in fur. Black, slimy hair hid the monster's face, except for its two red, glowing eyes. The second creature was as tall as Oscar, but bone thin. It walked proudly with featherless wings extended and head held high. The third demon looked human from the neck down and even had on a suit. However, its head was five times too big. Its large mouth could hold a normal-sized head, and its long, steel teeth looked as if they could easily bite one off.

After shaking hands and saying something to the old man with the angel, Tanas sat to his right at the desk across the four foot aisle. The old man's angel stood its ground against Tanas's demons. He never spoke, but when the angel's eyes flashed white, the demons backed away from the old man to stand on the far side of Tanas's desk.

***

Two hours of speech making wiped Sam out by noon. He tried to understand what they were talking about, but he eventually tuned them out. Most of the senators had left for lunch, including Tanas, so he leaned back in his cushioned chair.

"I wish we could get closer," he said, stretching.

"I've been thinking about that," said Abby, still leaning over the rail. "I might know a way." She pointed into the chamber.

Sam sat up straight.

"All those young people running errands for the senators get to walk the floor. We need to get our hands on their uniforms."

He looked over the railing. "They're older than us."

"Yeah, but I doubt anyone would notice. The guy at the door barely checks their badges."

Sam shook his head. "I kind of doubt they will give us their clothes. How are we supposed to get them?"

Abby narrowed her eyes in frustration. "I can't think of everything."

Something caught his eye on the chamber floor. Any other person would have seen a young man in a business suit walking down an aisle, but Sam saw the demon inside him. Most of the time, he could spot a possession by the dark shadow cast on the person. He'd missed Peony's because of the dark lighting in her shack. However, given enough time, the demon will eventually show itself. Here, the demon's face briefly merged with the host, causing the facial features of the man to blur.

The man did something odd when he passed Tanas's empty desk. Without pausing or even bending over, he dropped the briefcase in his hand. It came to rest neatly to the left of Tanas's desk. It was suspicious how the old man, only a few feet away, started choking on his lunch. It not only kept him from noticing the drop, but it also distracted the old man's angel.

Sam patted Abby's shoulder. "Hey, did you see him?"

"What?" Abby started scanning the chamber more thoroughly.

"He's standing at the bottom of the podium. He just turned to face us."

"Yeah, why?"

The man appeared to be smiling right at Sam. His first instinct was to duck, but the man's head turned a few degrees and then again. Sam followed his gaze. "He's smiling at the cameras."

"Why would he do that?" Abby shook her head as if confused.

"He dropped a briefcase at Tanas's desk, and now he's looking at the cameras. Whatever's in that briefcase, he wants credit for dropping it there."

The man straightened his tie, and for a second, the demon's face appeared. "That's so freaking creepy," Sam said, shivering.

"What?"

"He's possessed, and the demon's laughing."

"What do you think is in the briefcase?"

"I don't know, but it can't be good."

"Tanas has demons, right?"

"Yeah, three nasty ones." He shivered.

"Well, he might be running errands for Tanas. He did deliver the briefcase to his desk."

"No, it's something bad. He dropped off the briefcase real slick like."

The possessed man walked a different route back toward the exit.

Eli was right. He had no doubt what he should do next. "We need to follow him."

17—SENATOR TANAS

Sam and Abby exited the stairs as the possessed man came through the chamber doors. The crowded common area made it easy to follow him unnoticed. Abby pointed out Tanas and the six senators who had only demons, standing in the middle of the floor talking. Sam gaped at Abby in surprise when the man veered his course away from the group.

The man seemed in a hurry to get away from the evil group and didn't notice the spilled drink on the floor. His feet slipped out from under him, and his head struck the floor with a sickening crack. The demon sat up from the dazed man's body, nodded in Tanas's direction, and then left without his host. Tanas had his back turned, but his demons caught what happened. The bat-winged demon whispered in Tanas's ear. Tanas said something to the group and they all headed into the chamber, except for him. He and his demons headed for the young man.

Several people had come to the aid of the young man, who attempted to regain his feet. Tanas held out his well-manicured hand for help. "Harold, I hope you're all right. You took a nasty fall."

Harold obviously didn't know he had grabbed Tanas's hand because when his head came up he jerked back so hard he almost fell again. "I wouldn't be surprised if *you* spilled that drink on purpose."

Tanas chuckled lightly and addressed the small crowd more than Harold. "That's a bit paranoid, don't you think?"

"I know what your plans are, and I'll do whatever it takes to stop you." Harold's loud claim started to draw considerable attention. A security guard started walking in their direction.

Tanas opened his hands and shrugged in a gesture of innocence. "I'm sure you didn't mean to threaten me. Your head injury has you confused. Guard, this man needs to get checked out at the hospital."

The guard put one hand on Harold's arm in concern, but Harold jerked away, causing the crowd to gasp. "I don't need any help. I'm perfectly fine."

Tanas addressed the crowd. "There is no need for violence. We are all just concerned about you. Lunch is almost over. Do you want me to get your father before the session begins?" His fake concern made Sam's blood boil.

Harold looked at his own watch, frowning at the display. His mouth dropped open when he checked the clock on the wall. "This can't be. It should be ten o'clock."

"Ah, you confirmed our fears." Tanas held out his own watch for Harold. "It's well past ten. Now, be a good lad and let this fine officer get you some much needed help."

Harold's eyes darted around the growing crowd like a frightened child's. He didn't resist this time when the officer grabbed his arm and started escorting him away.

Before the crowd had a chance to disperse, Tanas spoke. "I'm sure Harold will be fine. There's no sense in spreading rumors about him threatening my life. That would be an injustice to him and his father, Senator Weinstein. Let's forget this ever happened and wish Harold our best."

One young lady in the crowd clapped at his words. Sam tried to keep from throwing up. The sweet-as-honey words were vials of poison that would spread the disease of gossip instead of stopping it. Sam gritted his teeth. "We have to check out that briefcase."

Abby pointed to a boy on a bench. "There's a senator's page. Let's go talk to him."

The boy was young but still a couple years older than Sam. He figured the page was worth checking out, so they both headed that way. The boy had his elbows resting on his thighs, his head hung low. When he moaned, Sam stopped Abby a few yards in front of the boy. He turned her so she would have her back to him. "I think he's sick," he whispered, peering over Abby's shoulder.

Sweat streamed from the boy's brow and dripped off the tip of his nose. He wiped his forehead with his palm, loosened his tie, and took off his jacket. The boy jerked upright, clutched his stomach, and ran for the bathroom. Sam walked over to the bench and sat down. Glancing around once, he put on the boy's jacket as if it were his own. When he checked the name badge, he smiled. "Trevor Krakowski." He held out the badge. "This can't be a coincidence. I'm Senator Weinstein's page. There's one. Now let's get you one."

The session must have started because the common area was almost empty—and no pages.

"I don't think I'm supposed to go." Abby straightened his tie. "Your pants don't match the jacket, but the badge should get you in."

Can you still read my thoughts when you're a human?

Abby grinned. "Of course," she said aloud and then continued in his head. "And you can still hear mine."

"Perfect," said Sam, grinning. "I won't be alone."

"Not as long as I'm around, you won't. Now, figure out what to do so we can go home. I'll be upstairs watching."

The guard at the door barely glanced at his name badge when he walked into the senate chamber. A few pages stood in the back, but they hardly gave him a second glance. He edged up to a tall blond girl holding a folder. "Which one is Senator Weinstein?" he asked, surveying the room.

He wasn't surprised to find her pointing at the old man with the angel. Several pages ran about, handing off papers or picking them up, but a few stood by their senators. Across the aisle from the old senator sat Tanas. His smug expression annoyed Sam, yet a tinge of fear kept him from moving.

Taking a deep breath, Sam headed down the aisle. Senator Weinstein was reading from a stack of papers when he stepped neatly behind him. He hoped the old man was too busy to notice.

"Ah, Trevor, you've returned. Are you feeling any better?" The old man turned to face Sam. His eyes squinted a bit, and then he lowered his glasses.

The angel glanced at the badge on Sam's jacket, frowning.

"I'm only here to help," Sam said, staring straight into the angel's face and nodding. His stomach clenched, waiting for the angel to make up his mind.

The angel waved his hand over the old man's eyes.

"Of course you are," the senator said, smiling. He took off his glasses, gave each lens a lick with his tongue, and started cleaning them with his sleeve. "All this reading is making me see things. Well, glad you're doing better. I'll have an errand for you after Senator Tanas speaks." He turned to his desk and started reading again.

"Can you hear me?" asked the angel in a deep low voice.

Sam nodded with his eyes forward.

"Is the senator in danger?"

Sam nodded and glanced down and to the right where the briefcase sat next to Tanas's desk.

The angel followed his eyes. "Something's in the case?"

Sam whispered, "Something bad."

"What's that?" Senator Weinstein jerked around. "What's bad?"

"Nothing, sorry. I didn't mean to disturb you." Sam's smile was weak, but it was enough to satisfy the old man.

The angel's eyes flashed white at the briefcase, and that's when Tanas's demons attacked.

Sam was used to seeing angels and demons walk through solid objects and even people. He had always assumed they couldn't touch each other, but he was horribly wrong. The fight was real and wicked. The angel managed to punch the hairy demon back, but the bat-winged demon clawed the angel's suit right off his back, along with giant chunks of skin. Angel blood squirted across Sam's face. Although he couldn't feel the blood, nor could anyone else see it, he still winced. He had to focus to stand still.

Abby, the angel and Tanas's demons are fighting.

"What caused the fight?"

I told the angel about the briefcase, and when he looked at it, the demons attacked.

"I can turn into a dog, grab the briefcase, and run out. They wouldn't do anything to a cute dog on the loose."

No, I need to find out what's inside first. It could kill you if it's bad.

"You're the one I'm worried about. My job is to protect you. If you think I'm going to stand here and let you get hurt, you're wrong."

Have a little faith. Stay where you are.

The angel held his own, but three against one took its toll. The demons obviously didn't want him near the case. Sam pictured the case opening with his mind. He almost jumped for joy when the latches flipped open. When the lid dropped to the floor, he almost jumped for another reason. Fear. His chazah gave him a terrible warning. He had only seconds to save the old man from the bomb. It barely registered when Tanas's name came over the loudspeaker. Tanas briskly rose from his chair and made his way toward the podium. Sam's lips turned into a snarl as he realized Tanas was getting out of the blast zone. Sam caught movement to the right. The blond page was coming down the aisle at exactly the wrong time. His first instinct was to shield the senator by tackling him away from the bomb, but if he did, the girl would die. For some reason, Oscar's words echoed in his head. *"Trust yer heart."*

I have to save both!

Sam formed a mental picture of Senator Weinstein thrown to safety, while he turned and ran for the pretty girl. The deafening bomb exploded as he tackled her to the floor.

His back burned in searing pain. He quickly rolled off her and jumped up. Her eyes were big from fear, but she didn't appear to be injured. "Are you OK?"

She nodded, and he helped her up. The alarms joined the many screams and yells echoing in the chamber as people stampeded for the doors. Sam's heart raced in fear as he searched through the smoke and debris for the senator. He had only practiced his telekinesis on a coin. He hoped with all his heart that his gift was strong enough to move a man. Twenty feet away from his chair, Senator Weinstein was trying to get up from the floor. Sam smiled as he helped the old man to his feet.

The old man squinted at Sam. "Trevor, are you all right?"

Sam grinned wide. "Yes, sir, I'm fine."

"How in the world did you throw me that far?" With the help of Sam, the old man carefully made his way through the debris.

"Just scared, I guess."

The blond page stood where he had left her.

"Well, don't just stand there. Help the senator to safety." Sam shook his head because his words sounded like something Eli would say.

The blonde broke out of her daze. "Oh yes. Senator, this way." She led him up the aisle.

The senator's angel, tattered from his fight, fell in behind them. He smiled a little when the battered angel gave him a nod and then followed the old man out of the chamber.

The blast radius was small, mainly within fifteen feet of the briefcase. Tanas was the only other injured person. His demons stood a few paces behind him, laughing and yelling insults at Senator Weinstein's angel, but Sam noticed they were sporting multiple wounds themselves. Tanas lay in the aisle, moaning and cradling his bloody arm, which gave Sam pause. Lying before him was the man who killed his parents. Tanas was well out of the range of the blast when it went off, but here he was pretending to be hurt. His rage screamed for action. Instinctively, he reached for his knife, but he remembered BK was in the truck. Desperately, he searched the wreckage for a weapon and found a splintered desk leg about a foot long. Tanas's demons were paying Sam no attention, the evil senator hadn't yet looked up, and everyone else was exiting the chamber. Here was his chance to make Tanas pay.

He gripped the stake tight, but his legs wouldn't move. Countless times he'd fantasized about Tanas's bloody end, and usually by his own hand, but this didn't feel right. He looked at his feet as if they had betrayed him, and tears filled his eyes as he dropped the stake to the floor. Yes, he hated Tanas. Yes, he wanted to kill him, and that's exactly why he couldn't.

Surprisingly, Oscar's words flooded his mind again. *"Follow yer heart."* Tanas would answer for his crimes, but not like this, not in cold blood. Sam wiped his eyes with his sleeve, turned from Tanas, and walked up the aisle as if he weren't there.

Abby's voice cut through the chaos. "Sam! Are you OK?"

Yeah, I'll meet you at the—

Before he finished the thought, she had her paws on his chest, licking him.

"Couldn't wait to turn back, huh?" Sam hugged his friend before letting her drop to the floor.

She hung her head as if she were in trouble. "I was getting ready to grab the case. It's my job to keep you safe."

Sam nodded and smiled. "I wouldn't want anyone else for the job."

A fireman and several men in suits with wires in their ears came rushing in as they were leaving.

"Are you injured?" asked the fireman, who then gave Abby a questioning glance.

"No, I'm OK," replied Sam, staring through him as if he couldn't see, "but I'm not sure about my guide dog." He reached down as if searching for her with his hand. "Is she OK?"

The fireman guided Sam's hand to Abby. "She seems fine to me. That's a special dog to stay with you through this."

"You have no idea," said Sam, smiling. "Come on, Abby. Let's get out of here."

"Nice one." She pretended to guide him out of the chamber.

Once they entered the common area, Sam laid the smoldering jacket on the bench. The common area was full of emergency workers steering people out of the building. Although some serious people were asking bystanders questions, they ignored the blind boy and his dog.

***

Eli stood waiting in the spot where they got the passes. He didn't say a word, but he had both eyebrows raised in expectation.

"We did it," Sam said, smiling.

Eli frowned and turned him around by the shoulders. "Maybe we should stop and let Penny heal those wounds.

They're not too bad, but if we let her, we won't have to stop training." Eli turned him back around, grinning. "This time, don't call her Ma. It makes her cranky."

"I don't know, Pa. Everything makes Ma cranky."

Eli chuckled and put his hand on Sam's shoulder. "You got a point, *son*. Now tell me about your adventure. I bet it's a dandy."

Sam's heart grinned so wide it hurt.

18—WOUNDED HERO

Sam rushed to tell Eli everything, except his temptation to finish Tanas off for good, before they met up with Dr. Prawn. Sam tried his best to mimic Eli's master storytelling style and, to his delight, got a couple of oohs and aahs from his stoic guardian. He figured Eli was adding on a bit for encouragement, but either way, Sam couldn't stop grinning.

Dr. Prawn and Oscar met them on the outskirts of DC in a vacant parking lot. It didn't take Dr. Prawn two seconds to heal the burns on his back, so he began retelling the story for them. There was no doubt about Oscar's excitement. He stomped his feet and swatted Sam's newly healed back throughout. He even winked when Sam mentioned that he followed his heart when he took a chance on saving both the senator and the page. However, Dr. Prawn's reaction was much less satisfying and even a little disturbing.

At the beginning of his story, her frown almost made a straight line, which was fantastic for her. However, when he finished his tale, her frown was deeper than ever. He hadn't called her "Ma," so it didn't make sense why she acted this way. It shouldn't have been a big deal, but her silent reaction felt like the sting of a poison dart.

Dr. Prawn's triangle-shaped head and bulbous eyes resembled a praying mantis as she cocked her head sideways. "If Senator Tanas was behind the bombing, why do you suppose he allowed himself to be injured?"

Sam clenched his jaw at her maddening stare. "The bomb was dropped at his desk by a possessed man. He had to be behind it."

"From your story, Harold Weinstein's demon nodded toward Tanas's demons before leaving. That could indicate Tanas was involved, but there are many other possibilities you're ignoring. Only weak minds believe what they want and don't search for the truth."

Unlike his insides, Sam was very calm in reply. "What other truth could there be? Tanas has demons, Harold was possessed, and the bomb was delivered to Tanas's desk."

Dr. Prawn shook her head and snarled her lip as if disgusted at his response. "That's exactly my point. Why would he bomb himself?"

Sam looked around for help, but everyone was silent, waiting for his reply. His heart pounding in his ears made thinking difficult. "Tanas was getting up to speak. Maybe he didn't plan on being at his desk when it went off."

She rubbed her pointed chin with her thumb and forefinger in thought. "Possibly, but that would mean he made a foolish mistake. Tanas could be called many things, but I doubt foolish is one of them."

Sam wouldn't throw out another theory for her to shoot down. She obviously thought he was stupid and was getting enjoyment out of proving it true. He very much wanted to give her a swift kick to the shins, but he decided to shrug his shoulders and head for the truck.

Prawn's poisonous remarks not only sucked the joy from him, it also affected Eli. So much so, he had Sam repeat the story in detail on the way home. As he finished the story for the third time, his enthusiasm for the telling had considerably waned.

It just didn't make sense. He was sure Tanas was behind the bombing, but why would he allow himself to be injured? When the evening news came on, all three sat on the edge of their seats. He wasn't the only one hoping for answers.

Sam stifled a grin when the news reporter interviewed the blond page. "Trevor must have seen the bomb because he shoved the senator out of the way, and then he dove on me. He saved our lives."

The reporter cut over to Senator Weinstein. "Yes, Trevor is a hero in my book. If he hadn't thrown me out of the way, I'm sure I would've been killed." The senator was sincere, but the feisty old codger was gone, and a beaten man had replaced him. Sam sadly smiled when he noticed the senator's angel holding him up.

The real Trevor had his jacket on when they interviewed him. "I don't remember anything other than being sick in the bathroom." The reporter made light of his apparent humility, branding him a true hero. "Seriously, I don't remember a thing."

The next segment cut to a solemn reporter in front of the hospital. She gave the grim news about how serious Tanas's injuries were, but there was hope he could still pull through. The report ended with the grave newsperson gazing dramatically toward the hospital.

"What a load of baloney. He was barely scratched." Eli's raised hand forced Sam to shut up.

A video started, showing several men in uniforms escorting Harold Weinstein off in handcuffs. "Based on the surveillance cameras in the chamber, Harold Weinstein, son of Senator Weinstein, was arrested for the bombing. Eyewitnesses stated Harold had to be removed from the Capitol only minutes before the bombing after threatening Senator Tanas's life."

Sam recognized the woman who had the microphone stuck in her face. She was the one who had clapped after Tanas's speech in the common area. "I don't know why, but Harold said he would kill Senator Tanas."

Sam slapped his forehead in frustration. "Harold didn't say he'd kill him. He said he'd stop him. Tanas put that in her head."

Eli shushed him, and Sam's lips pressed tightly.

The reporter continued. "Based on his son's involvement in the terrible incident, Senator Weinstein announced his retirement from the US Senate. He plans to work full time helping his son through his mental break."

"He didn't have a mental break. He had a demon." Sam threw his hands up in frustration.

"Quiet, we're getting to it now." Eli leaned closer to the TV.

"Senator Weinstein's retirement will leave the chairman position open for the Committee on Appropriations. As we all know, this powerful committee holds the government's purse strings. With the sentiment for being wounded so heinously during his act of service to our country, senator Tanas is the hands-down favorite to step into the chairman position, if he pulls through."

Eli turned off the TV, shaking his head in disgust.

"They got it all wrong," said Sam, standing up. "Maybe we should go and set those idiot reporters straight."

Eli turned to Sam. "What can you tell them that they'll believe?"

Sam had lots of experience with people not believing the truth. He sighed and sat back down on the couch. "Not one thing."

"Tanas is evil—but smart. He set Harold up good and made himself out to be the wounded hero. He probably intended to kill Senator Weinstein, but it still worked out for him by setting up the son. He always intended to be injured, and he'll milk his injuries for all they're worth. I'd bet my life he or someone under his control has the gift of healing. That reporter did get one thing right. He'll get the chairman spot."

Sam felt as if someone had kicked him in the stomach. "So, I failed." *I should have killed him when I had the chance.* In his fury, he had neglected to keep Abby out of his head. She whined, obviously disliking his thoughts, but she showed no signs of letting Eli know what he was thinking.

"You didn't fail. You did exactly what you were supposed to do. You saved two innocent lives. Tanas's plans were only the circumstances."

"But Tanas got everything he wanted." Sam punched the couch.

Abby nuzzled him. "Sam, only you can hear me. You need to tell Eli the whole story." Her kiss to his cheek made his head swivel in surprise. For just a moment, it felt human, but she was still in dog form. His heart raced as he prepared to tell his secret.

"Eli, I left part of the story out."

Eli responded by sitting back in his chair, staring blankly.

"After the bomb and before I left the chamber, Tanas was hurt on the floor. I grabbed a splintered desk leg and had full intentions of driving it through his black heart."

No emotion crossed Eli's face. "Why didn't you?"

"I wanted to. I wanted to super bad, but I just couldn't. My chest burned like the day you told me he killed my parents, but thinking about killing him this way made my heart feel as if it were ripping from my chest. I dropped the stake and left."

Eli sat in silence a good long while before he spoke. "I know why *you* were given this task. This was a test. If you had succumbed to hate and killed Tanas, you would have failed. No doubt you would have lost all your powers and I probably would be waiting another thousand years for a replacement."

"But if I had killed him, you wouldn't need a replacement because he'd be gone."

Eli gave a sad chuckle. "No, Tanas is a man. If he died, evil would find someone new to do its bidding. Do you think his three demons would just sit on a stump and say 'The game's over. Let's be good now'?"

"Probably not, but Tanas still got what he wanted."

"He did today, but something tells me he won't always as long as you're around." Eli slapped Sam on the leg. "Now cheer up. That pretty girl you saved will have a chance to grow up, have a family, and be happy. If you hadn't been there, that girl would have died for sure."

Abby put her feet on his lap. "Yeah, you did great. But, as far as the girl goes, I didn't think she was that pretty." She ducked her head.

"Not as pretty as you, anyway." Sam scratched his friend behind her hound ears and then leaned in to kiss her droopy nose. He pictured her in human form, and his temperature rose a few degrees. "Dog or human, you've got her beat, easy."

Abby giggled and gave him an affectionate swipe of her tongue. "At least you have good taste."

Eli stood up and pulled an envelope from his back pocket. "I almost forgot. Oscar told me to give you this at bedtime." Eli handed it over to Sam. "It's sealed, so I guess it's private, but I'm really curious what it is, if you want to share." Eli made no attempt to hide his desire to see what was in the letter as he hovered over Sam.

Sam, curious himself, wasted no time ripping it open. It was a rather curious letter, but nothing he couldn't share, so he read it aloud for Eli and Abby.

"The Wolves Within"

Unknown Author

An old grandfather said to his grandson, who came to him with anger at a friend who had done him an injustice, "Let me tell you a story.

"I, too, at times, have felt a great hate for those that have taken so much, with no sorrow for what they do. But hate wears you down and does not hurt your enemy. It is like taking poison and wishing your enemy would die. I have struggled with these feelings many times."

He continued, "It is as if there are two wolves inside me. One is good and does no harm. He lives in harmony with all around him and does not take offense when no offense was intended. He will only fight when it is right to do so, and in the right way.

"But the other wolf, ah! He is full of anger. The littlest thing will set him into a fit of temper. He fights everyone, all the time, for no reason. He cannot think because his anger and hate are so great. It is helpless anger, for his anger will change nothing. Sometimes, it is hard to live with these two wolves inside me, for both of them try to dominate my spirit."

The boy looked intently into his grandfather's eyes and asked, "Which one wins, Grandfather?"

The grandfather smiled and quietly said, "The one I feed."

Above all else, guard your heart, for everything you do flows from it.

Well done, Sam!

    Your humble servant,

Oscar

"Well, I'll be," Eli said, grinning. "That's an old Native American story. Oscar is full of surprises. He hit the nail on the head with that one. I wonder how he knew you passed the test."

Sam didn't know, but reading Oscar's letter drained every bad feeling he had, leaving only joy.

Eli crossed his arms. "Time for bed, training tomorrow."

"Awww, come on, Pa. Can't you give us a break?" Sam smiled with hope.

Eli grimly looked down. "You passed the test this time, but if you ever expect to truly beat evil, we have a lot of work to make you the Grand Master of the Knights Templar."

Sam looked up, just as grim. "I'll have breakfast ready."

Eli turned and walked to his room. "I never had a doubt."

Cozy in his bed with Abby warmly snuggled against him, Sam was using his telekinesis to hover Oscar's letter and his favorite picture of his folks above his head. His eyes floated dreamily back and forth between the two. He had come a long way since his days in the group home. All his hard work had paid off, but he still had a long way to go. Although he would have preferred ruining Tanas's plans completely, he at least saved the girl's and the senator's lives. Not to mention passing the test. His eyes kept going to the one line on Oscar's letter. *Well done, Sam!*

The story Oscar told in his letter also helped him to better understand what he had been feeling inside. It's not an all-or-nothing deal. There will always be good and bad inside everyone. The trick is to focus on the good more than the bad. It sounded easy, but Sam knew it was going to be hard. He came very close to failing today. Just the thought of Tanas made his blood boil, but he was determined for the good wolf inside him to overcome.

Sam was about to drift off when new words suddenly appeared at the bottom of Oscar's letter. His eyes popped open and he grabbed the letter with his hands, but when he did, the words disappeared. He shook the cobwebs from his head, but the words were still gone. He could've sworn they said:

I have faith in you.

ABOUT THE AUTHOR

http://www.rssexton.com/